"A tense, dramatic story of pursuit, raw hate and primitive love."—*Atlanta Journal*

"A gripping novel and an impressive study of character... A fine story told with excitement."—*Charleston News & Courier*

"Full of suspense, drama and good characterization."—*Hollywood Citizen News*

"Three people on a raft, two convicts with a beautiful, underprivileged girl between them, move across the surface of a flood, beset by passion and hate, by fear and a vow of vengeance, moving unerringly, toward a hidden destiny..."—*Montgomery Advertiser*

"The floods are of water as well as fear, and the Hawkins team has done here a strong and dramatic novel of suspense."
—*Raleigh News Observe*

"Against an excellent background, a winter flood reminiscent of last Winter's calamity around Yuba City, the Hawkinses have set a melodrama... moments of genuine suspense... descriptions magnificent."
—*San Francisco Chronicle*

"Well-crafted revenge novel with an ethical core."—Bill Kelly

John & Ward Hawkins Bibliography
(1910-1978) (1912-1990)

Novels:
As by John & Ward Hawkins:
We Will Meet Again (Dial Press, 1940)
Secret Command (Novel Selections, 1943)
Pilebuck (Dutton, 1943)
Broken River (Dutton, 1944)
Devil on His Trail (Dutton, 1944)
If I Kill Him (Handi-Books, 1945)
The Floods of Fear (Dodd, Mead, 1956;
  reprinted as *A Girl, a Man, and a River*, 1957)
Violent City (Dodd, Mead, 1957)
Death Watch (Dodd, Mead, 1958)
Frame-Up on the Highway (Scott, Foresman, 1963)

As by John Hawkins
Arc of Fire (Famous Fantastic Mysteries, 1943)

As by Ward Hawkins:
Kings Will Be Tyrants (McGraw-Hill, 1959)
The Damnation of John Doyle Lee (Tara Press, 1982)

Harry Borg & Guss series:
Sword of Fire (Del Rey, 1985)
Red Flame Burning (Del Rey, 1985)
Blaze of Wrath (Del Rey, 1986)
Torch of Fear (Del Rey, 1987)

THE FLOODS OF FEAR

By John & Ward Hawkins

Black Gat Books • Eureka California

THE FLOODS OF FEAR

Published by Black Gat Books
A division of Stark House Press
1315 H Street
Eureka, CA 95501, USA
griffinskye3@sbcglobal.net
www.starkhousepress.com

THE FLOODS OF FEAR
Originally published in hardback by Dodd, Mead & Co., Inc,
New York, and copyright © 1956 by The Curtis Publishing
Company; John and Ward Hawkins. Reprinted in paperback by
Popular Library, New York, 1957 as A Girl, a Man, and a River.
First serialized in the Saturday Evening Post, 1956.

Copyright © 2024 Stark House Press. All rights reserved under
International and Pan-American Copyright Conventions.

ISBN: 979-8-88601-073-2

Cover design by Jeff Vorzimmer, ¡caliente!design, Austin, Texas
Text design by Mark Shepard, shepgraphics.com
Proofreading by Bill Kelly

PUBLISHER'S NOTE:
This is a work of fiction. Names, characters, places and
incidents are either the products of the author's imagination or
used fictionally, and any resemblance to actual persons, living
or dead, events or locales, is entirely coincidental.
Without limiting the rights under copyright reserved above, no
part of this publication may be reproduced, stored, or
introduced into a retrieval system or transmitted in any form
or by any means (electronic, mechanical, photocopying,
recording or otherwise) without the prior written permission of
both the copyright owner and the above publisher of the book.

First Stark House Press/Black Gat Edition: February 2024

CHAPTER ONE

Spring had been late this year. Early rains had drenched the coastal lands, but static cold held the high country locked in a frozen grip. Daily reports from a hundred sources came to the headquarters of the Corps of Engineers. Snow depth, mean temperatures, rainfall and water levels. The men who tabulated them had to go deep into the files to find a year when the big river and its tributary streams had been so low in April.

May was a month of waiting. Warm rains fell in the first week of June. White water foamed in the streams on the lower mountain slopes. The Charles River began to rise, then the Black Fork, the Elk. The big river nudged at the gauge floats—lazily, as if testing its strength. Everywhere in the high country, all at once, the runoff began. The Charles left its banks to drown a dairy farmer in his bed. The rampaging Black Fork swept half a dozen bridges from their piers. Flood gauges on the Elk and Clear Water jumped wildly upward. A day later, the big river smashed a dike and wrecked a grange hall, two farmhouses and a crossroads store.

Greenfield, at the foot of the mountains, the inland terminus of navigable water, was the first city to feel the brunt of the flood. Houseboats and boathouses and pleasure craft were torn from their moorings. The pavement of Main Street was under water. Crest estimates were revised upward almost hourly.

Downstream, all along the big river, the machinery of state and local government was moving, crash priority. Engineers studied maps of the big river—predicted crest, plus or minus dike top elevation—and marked the dikes that could not be saved. Evacuation of low-lying areas was begun. Construction crews moved in to strengthen the dikes that might be held. Labor gangs were recruited on the streets of all the river towns and cities—farmers, clerks, mechanics, high school boys—anyone and everyone who could use a shovel or carry a sandbag.

There weren't enough men available to do the work that had to be done. Below Greenfield, a ten-mile stretch of dike collapsed in a dozen places. A convoy of trucks was caught, still loading, in Frenchman's Glen, and the known flood dead topped the hundred mark. Other evacuations did not go as planned. Some people flatly refused to leave their homes. Others returned to guard their possessions, cutting across fields and through wood lots to avoid police roadblocks.

There weren't enough men, though city and county jails were opened and the most dependable prisoners thrown into the fight. Every hour was important. An hour gained, a dike held firm against the flood's onslaught for even an hour, meant an incalculable saving in lives and property. Hard-pressed officials in Lebannon, next in the flood's path, turned to the state prison there for help. Men from the honor farm worked beside the citizens of the town. Then the trustees were recruited. Finally, prison officials asked for volunteers from the heavy labor gangs, the convicts who normally spent their days building the prison annex.

These were the shock troops. Expendable, though the word was never used. The incorrigibles and those who had attempted escape were screened from the volunteers. Those remaining were told off in twelve-man crews, an armed sergeant assigned to each crew. Trucks rolled north through Lebannon before daylight, taking them to the trouble spots. Tom Sharkey's crew was dropped near the midpoint of the Humboldt dike, where wind and weather had damaged its earthen bulk. Greenfield and Bridgeton were above them. Lebannon was ten miles downriver. Lebannon, huddled under the ridges, was already in trouble and the crest was an estimated thirty or forty hours away. Below Lebannon, the big river was tearing at the dikes of West Mills, Biddleford and Franklin.

Tom Sharkey's crew worked in a driving rain. Twelve men, wearing square-billed caps, brogans and gray prison denim, so mud-smeared the numbers stenciled on their shirts could not be read. They were a fair cross section of the population of the prison—a forger, car thieves, burglars, a safe man, a molester, a man who'd specialized in armed robbery and a convicted murderer serving a life term. They filled and placed sandbags, watched by the silent Sharkey who wore a slicker and rubber boots and carried a .30-30 rifle in the crook of his arm.

The big and swollen river was east of them. Drift and wreckage rode the breast of it—logs and timbers, clumps of uprooted brush and trees, a shed roof, an overturned skiff, and something deeply awash that might have been a house. A red raft that had once been a barn door passed close by, spinning slowly, ridden by a shivering dog. Some of the convicts halted work to shout encouragement. Doc Barr—three-time loser, five years served, four years to go—asked Tom Sharkey to use his rifle.

"Put him out of his misery."

"He'll make it," Sharkey said. "He can swim."

"More'n I can do," Doc Barr said.

There was a road of sorts atop the dike. Dump trucks brought sand and sacks. At noon, food came—sandwiches wrapped in waxed paper, cold coffee in a gallon jug. Tom Sharkey didn't eat. A man who had only to stand and hold a rifle and keep a nose count can skip a meal or two. He tossed his lunch to the men and saw his sandwiches torn by muddy hands, the pieces passed around, one extra bite for every man.

"Okay," he said. "Back to work."

The Humboldt country was west of them, below the dike—truck farms, dairy and orchard land. The north-south highway lay to the west, half a mile from the dike, a long mile or more from the hills they could dimly see through the blowing rain. All morning the highway had been clogged: a parade of police and army vehicles, private trucks and cars. After lunch, only the dump trucks were moving on the roads down there, scooting across the bottom land, bringing sand and sacks to the men who fought the rising river.

"Y'notice," said Shorty Kniss, forger. "They ain't in much hurry to get there, but they're hell for gettin' back."

"Less talk," Tom Sharkey said. "More work."

Four men filled sacks, alternating on the shovels. Two men were the wire-and-lift team; in turn they bent a bit of wire around a sack top, together they heaved it up—"Hip! Ho!"—to the shoulder of the man who was waiting for the load, feet spread and braced. Six men were packers, the mules, slipping and floundering away to add another bag to the wall of sandbags on the river face of the dike.

The day wore on. The twelve convicts filled and wired and placed the sacks, moving heavily, steam rising from their sodden clothes. At dusk, a dump truck appeared with a gasoline generator in tow. A mechanic climbed out of the cab to show Tom Sharkey how to start the motor and switch on the floodlight.

"We'll need food and drinking water," Sharkey said.

The mechanic said, "I'll pass the word."

Doc Barr said, "Make mine pheasant under glass."

Darkness came. Tom Sharkey stood in the shadow beside the bellowing generator, watching and counting the tired men. "Truck coming," someone yelled. The bag fillers, the wire-and-lift team moved out of the dump area into the full glare of the floodlight where they would stand until the truck had gone. Tom Sharkey's thumb found the safety button above the rifle's trigger. In eighteen years of service he had never lost a prisoner; he didn't intend to lose one now. The truck howled backward out of the night, hoist squealing.

"Ask him," Kniss yelled. "Where's the chow?"

"It'll be here," Sharkey said. "This truck or next."

"Don't count on it," a deep voice said.

This was Bruce Donavan, the murderer. He was one of the packers, standing a little apart from the others, hands loose at his sides. He was a tall man, big of shoulder, deep of chest—no flat-bellied beauty, this one. He was thick-waisted, his heavy torso set on heavy thighs. His hands and feet were big. His face was brown, dirty now. He had a short, straight nose, brown eyes, a stubborn jaw. His muddy rag of shirt was open upon a hairless chest. His pants were rolled to the knee, his feet were bare.

"Donavan," Sharkey said. "Where're your shoes?"

"I took them off."

"So I see," Sharkey said. "Why?"

"It's getting along to that time."

Now the dump truck jolted to a stop, hoist whining. The tailgate opened and wet sand spilled out. Sharkey left his place beside the generator to ask the driver about food. "I wouldn't know," the driver said. "I ain't had nothin' to eat myself since breakfast." He gunned the motor nervously. "I'll tell 'em what you said."

"Do that," Tom Sharkey said.

He stepped back and made a quick count: two men with shovels, two with bags, two who had wads of wire thrust under their belts. Donavan, the murderer, standing alone. He was always alone. Beyond Donavan, Peebles, the armed robbery, gun and knife specialist, steel-rimmed glasses glinting. Beyond Peebles, Dortch, Avent, Barr and Kniss, the other packers. Twelve men, all present and accounted for. Sharkey lifted an arm in signal and the dump truck roared away, chasing its headlight glow up the dike.

"Move in," Sharkey said. "Let's go some more."

He stood beside the generator, back to the driving

rain. Shovels bit into the sand. A sack was filled and dragged along a mud-slick plank, wired shut. Donavan, the murderer, stepped up out of turn, feet braced, back bent, waiting for the load. The big guy was a fool for work, you had to give him that. All day he'd been passing the other packers on the path, doing more, doing twice as much as any other, without complaint. But he was one to watch, a question mark. He'd done six years of a life sentence, every day of it hard time. He'd done six years and had yet to make a friend of another con.

"Donavan," Sharkey said. "I want to talk to you."

"Next time around," Donavan said.

He went down the muddy path, the sandbag on his shoulder, moving easily, without haste. That, too, was Donavan. Any of the others would have jumped at the chance to fall out of line. Not Donavan. The big guy asked no favors, wanted none.

"Yes?" Donavan said.

His voice was pitched to carry above the generator's steady roar. He was standing in the glare of the light, a good six feet from Tom Sharkey. He had been trained to stand thus when reporting to a guard who held a rifle. He wasn't smiling. He rarely smiled, but his eyes could laugh at you.

"Why the bare feet?" Sharkey asked.

"I swim better that way."

"Don't try a dive. I'm a good wing shot."

"I won't have to dive."

"Still comin' up, eh? How fast?"

"Two inches an hour. Maybe three."

"It'll level off."

"No," Donavan said evenly. "It's time we left. It was time to leave three hours ago." Half the convict crew were listening now. "We can't fill enough sandbags to do any good."

"How do you know so much?"

"I used to build dikes on this river," Donavan said,

"and docks and wing dams and ferry slips. We can't save this one—the U.S. Army couldn't save it now. If you want to get these men back inside the walls, alive, you'd better put them aboard the next truck out."

"That'll do!" Sharkey said. "That's enough!"

Donavan, the murderer, turned on his heel. At the sand pile all work had ceased; the men were listening, rain-wet faces turned to the light. Peebles, the lean, tough thief who'd specialized in attack from behind, caught at Donavan's arm. Donavan brushed his hand away and bent to take a sandbag from the muddy plank.

"Hey!" Peebles said.

He grabbed at a bag not yet wired shut. He got it on his shoulder, unaided, and went floundering down the path after Donavan. The others began to move again, slowly, talking among themselves. Tom Sharkey's thumb found the safety above the rifle's trigger. It wasn't bad enough to be stuck out here without relief, no food, no drinking water. Now he had the making of panic on his hands.

Donavan dropped the sandbag atop the sloping wall of bags on the river face of the dike, then stood for a moment watching the suck and swirl of muddy water. Another foot ... two feet, and they were done. Perhaps even before the water reached the top the dike would go. The dike was earth and very old. Springs and seepage and burrowing animals must have weakened it in innumerable places. One of them would crumble suddenly. The face of the dike would crack and let the water in, and then the big river would rip and tear and devour.

"Hey!" Peebles said. "Hey, Donavan!"

Donavan said, "What do you want?"

"What you said—" Peebles pushed his mud-smeared glasses up on his forehead. "What you told the gun screw, were you on the level? Were you givin' it to him straight?"

"Yes," Donavan said.

"The dike's goin' to go, huh?"

"Yes," Donavan said.

"Holy Mother!" The words came at the end of Peebles breath. He turned to look back into the blue-white eye of the big floodlight. "He ain't goin' to take us out o' here—not without orders 'n' help, he ain't. He'll keep us here till he's got another gun screw an' a motorcycle bull to ride escort." He wiped his hands on his shirt. "What're we goin' to do?"

"I'm staying. Do whatever you like."

"I can swim some—" Peebles looked at the dark boil and froth of water along the face of the dike, looked out over the swollen river. "Not in that. Niagara Falls in a bucket, man. Ain't nobody goin' to swim in that."

"You've got a choice," Donavan said. "The rifle or the river."

"Some choice!" Peebles said.

A voice near the generator said, "Hey, look at this! We got a river inside the dike. And it's coming up fast!"

The water inside the dike was not yet a river. It was slack water, fed by seepage and minor breaks and the overflow of water backed into minor streams. But it covered a wide area. Out in the dark beyond the reach of their light, much of the flat land to the south and west already lay submerged, and in many places the water had covered the north-south highway. There were cars stalled along the highway, most all of them abandoned. Some of the owners had walked to safety, others had been picked up by trucks, still others had found high ground.

A few were still in their cars. Elizabeth Matthews and Carl Corbin were two of these. She was twenty-three, a post-graduate student at the University. Her parents and a brother and sister lived not far from the town of Biddleford. When she'd heard news reports saying the town of Biddleford was in danger she'd wanted immediately—and senselessly, she knew now—to be with her parents. Carl Corbin, nineteen, an undergraduate and a family friend, had agreed to drive her home. They'd come this far, to this depression in the road. Their car headlights showed them a sheet of still water covering the road. They had no way of knowing its width or depth.

"I'm afraid of it," Elizabeth said. She scrubbed mist from the windshield and peered past the beating windshield wipers. "In this ink, I can't tell if it's a puddle or a lake. What if we get stuck in the middle of it?"

"That we wouldn't like!" Carl said.

"Hadn't we better turn back?"

Carl's young face was twisted in hard thought. He tried to keep his own fear out of his voice. "We don't know what's back of us now. It might be as bad as this, or worse."

"I suppose you're right."

"We can't be far from Lebannon," he said. "I'd guess a mile, maybe two. If we can get there, we're safe. And even if we get stuck here I can hike on in and get a tow car. We'd do better to go ahead than to go back and get stuck in the middle of nowhere." He rolled the window down and peered into the driving rain. "It doesn't look too bad. I think I can see clear road on the other side." He turned to her. "Let's give it a try, Beth."

"You're the driver."

"So cross your fingers," he said.

He put the car in low gear and eased it forward into the water. They went perhaps twenty yards without trouble, though the sound of the water against the fenders was anything but a comfort. The sound changed, becoming muffled as the water deepened. Carl pulled himself up tight against the steering wheel, peering down over the hood. His young face was white and strained. Elizabeth's hands were clenched in aching fists.

"Carl, it's getting deeper!"

"You're telling me!"

He knew now the clear road he'd seen had been imagined. He was committed, and he was too young to change his mind quickly or willingly. They went on ... five yards, ten. The motor sputtered. Frightened, Carl shifted into second quickly and gunned the motor with the hope of bulling through. The motor stuttered and coughed and died. The starter whirred on and on without result.

Carl stared through the windshield. "I goofed ..."

"You tried," Elizabeth said. "It was a good try."

Carl opened the door. The water was level with the bottom of it. "A bloody lake," he said. He stood up, leaning on the door, holding to the car top. He could see nothing hopeful in the rain-laced darkness. He got back into the car, wiping his dripping face. "Looks like I go wading."

"Wading where?"

"Down the road. Lebannon can't be too far, but there should be help closer than that. A farmer with a truck or something. You'll be all right here."

"Can't I go with you?"

Carl got out of the car. The water was knee-deep. "In this?" he asked. He buttoned his coat against the rain. "Don't be a dope! I'll get wet enough for both of us. At least wait till I take a look down the road."

"Don't be gone long."

"Ten minutes," he said. "That's a promise. I'll find somebody, or I'll come back for you. And look—make like a lighthouse. Turn the lights on now and then and toot the horn. It's as dark as the inside of a goat out here. I don't want to lose you."

He closed the door and waded away. When he was beyond the reach of the lights, Elizabeth turned them off. She waited a few moments, then pulled the switch to turn them on again. They did not come on. And the horn was dead. Presently, the rising water was covering the floor inside the car. She lifted her feet up to the cushions. Carl did not come back in ten minutes, or in fifteen minutes. And not in a half hour.

The rising water drove Elizabeth out of the car. She climbed to the hood, then to the top. Standing in the darkness and the rain, shivering with the cold that soaked through her belted raincoat, she was a very frightened girl. But she tried not to be. She couldn't make like a lighthouse. She tried her best to make like a foghorn. Every moment or two she sent a wailing cry through the night.

Tom Sharkey stood beside the roaring generator, the rifle in his hands. He counted convicts, checking names against the roster in his mind. He'd picked those who were most dependable for the dump area jobs: bag filling, wire-and-lift. Schorer, a molester, big as an ox and just as dumb, was paired with Wilkes, a wiry stub of a man, a burglar. Witzel, a sneak thief, and Rudisill, who'd stripped and stolen cars, worked together. Turnidge, a big, blond kid, another car thief, was teamed with Regan, a sullen man who'd burned his neighbors' barns.

The packers were the men to watch. Tom Sharkey had deliberately given them the mule work; tired men don't have the strength to run. Some of them were nearing exhaustion now. Doc Barr, tavern burglar, had slipped and fallen twice. He'd had trouble getting up, but he hadn't asked for rest. Doc had a wife and daughter in Lebannon. "Pearl'll do all right," he'd said. "But Midge—hell, she's just a little bit of a thing, probably scared to death."

"Who ain't?" Shorty Kniss had said.

Shorty, a grinning ape with a scarred nose, was a forger, a man who got two drinks and started writing checks. "Sober, they'd never catch me," he'd said. "Trouble is, that's why I write the checks, so I c'n get real drunk." Shorty might panic, Sharkey thought, but he'd be the last to charge the gun. Dortch, a safe man, and Avent, armed robbery, were a different sort. They were prison-wise, old cons; their muddy faces told nothing of their thoughts. Both were big and strong, capable of almost anything. And there was Peebles, the worst of the lot. He'd gone the route—knife and gun and club. He wouldn't charge the rifle, but he'd be happy to come from behind with shovel, boots and fists, while someone else was getting shot. Now, for reasons of his own, he was slipping and floundering in the wake of Donavan, the murderer, trying desperately to keep up.

Tom Sharkey stood with his back against the gas tank of the generator, watching and counting the men. He could hear the voice of the river above the motor's sound, a kind of subdued and sullen muttering. On the river side of the dike it was within inches of the top, a powerful and ripping current. On the near side it was ten feet lower and still, but rising steadily. He knew it had covered much of the low farm land to the west and portions of the north-south highway. There'd been no car lights south of the truck turn-off for some time now, and the drivers coming down from the north had reported water across sections of the highway in that direction.

They were an unhappy lot, those drivers. They didn't try to hide their worry, or their fear. Some had dropped out. The intervals between trucks were longer now; the trucks that came dumped their loads of sand and ran, gears howling, down the dike and away. They brought no food. Worse, they brought no promise of relief. "We're at the bottom of the list," Peebles said. "They're tryin' to save everybody they can—all the good people. Who cares a damn about cons?"

"If it's us," Doc Barr said, "or a like number of old folks, women and kids, let it be us. And I say it's a good swap. What d'you say, Donavan?"

Donavan said, "I say you're right."

"Keep moving!" Tom Sharkey said.

As long as they were here they would do a job. They kept moving, but panic and exhaustion had slowed some of them. Half the packers were stumbling. Doc Barr fell again, and this time he could not get up until Donavan helped him to his feet. Donavan was naked to the waist. He'd shed his shirt and somehow ripped the legs of his trousers off, halfway between belt and knee.

"Donavan!" Sharkey said. "You tryin' to start a riot?"

"You know better," Donavan said.

He was still doing the work of two men, Peebles panting and scrambling in his wake. A dump truck came backward down the dike, hoist yelling, paused and roared away. Water was climbing the sandbags now, water was leaking through them. Donavan helped Doc Barr up the path and dropped him at Sharkey's feet.

"This one's done," he said.

"Wait!" The stiff turning of Sharkey's head told how much this effort cost. "How long've we got? When—?"

Donavan said, "We've run out of time."

He turned his back on Sharkey, moving past Avent, Dortch and Kniss to shoulder a sandbag. He walked the muddy path, listening and waiting, feeling the faint trembling of the earth beneath his feet. He placed the bag, another brick on an already failing wall. He wheeled and Peebles caught at his arm—a frantic Peebles, shirt and shoes gone, pants legs torn away. "Help me," Peebles said breathlessly. "Something happens, you got to help me, Donavan. I can't hardly swim at all."

"If I can," Donavan said.

A truck backed into the dump area, wildly spilling sand. The driver's face was white, his foot heavy on the throttle. And a new sound was on the wind, not loud, but rising steadily. Someone in the dump area yelled: "She's gone! Look inside!" Donavan saw water pouring into the lighted area, a roaring wall of water, fast lifting the inside level toward the river level. Gears clashed and the truck lurched away and the headlights found a muddy torrent pouring across the dike. The truck engine howled, the headlights swung and tipped and vanished utterly.

Now the dike beneath Donavan's feet shook and settled and water poured down the length of it. He heard screams and saw men, arms flailing desperately, stumble and fall and disappear under the water. He could not help them. He was still on his feet, but the shove of the current was hard against his hips, boiling up, building up against his back, sucking away below his legs. He saw the river take two more, Wilkes and Turnidge. They rode out of the light, looking fearfully downstream, heads held rigid and high. A third man, Dortch, went almost willingly into the water and did not reappear. Peebles' wild yelling was shrill and thin.

"Hang onto me! Give me a hand! I can't—"

Peebles' hands clawed at Donavan's wet and naked back. Donavan's arm went out to offer support. The current drove Peebles hard against Donavan, rolled him down the length of Donavan's arm. Donavan's reaching hand found only naked flesh and nothing to grip. Peebles went under water, then emerged downstream, paddling furiously, riding high.

Again the earth was cut from beneath Donavan. Now there were no inside and outside water levels; the two levels had met, becoming one, and the dike was slowly melting under it. Donavan staggered, but found new footing, bare feet braced against the coarse sacking of the sandbags. The water boiled over his shoulders. He turned to put the plane of his chest against the stream. There had been no one left on the melting dike downstream. Now, with the light he had, he could see only Tom Sharkey above.

The guard had managed what the others could not because the bulk of the generator was breaking the full strength of the current, giving him a boiling eddy to stand in, an anchor to cling to. His rifle was gone. He'd stripped off his raincoat and shirt, and he'd shed his boots. He was ready. The generator settled, tipping the light to a crazy slant, and Sharkey gave himself to the river, splashing out into it in the clumsy way of a man who can swim only a little. He passed beyond Donavan's reach. His bald head was awash, sinking and rising. There was no cry from him, no show of fear.

Now Donavan was alone. He stayed on, his leg muscles corded and hard with the strain, the water boiling up from his chest, drenching his face. He was not going to escape. Donavan, the murderer, was going to stay where the guard had left him until he was overpowered by the river. The generator gave way at last. The light wheeled across the rain-laced darkness, the motor roared and died and the light was gone. Donavan's feet began to slide. He had time to face downstream, to fill his lungs. He had to go, and he went as any man would go toward freedom. He dived with a powerful thrust that carried him very deep into the river and very far.

He didn't try to surface. He let the water have its way with him, tossing him, twisting him, buffeting him in a turmoil of conflicting currents. He was being carried swiftly downstream, but there was no sensation of being carried. The darkness was complete. He could feel only the fluid forces of the currents working on him, driving him up and down, hurling him from side to side. When his breath was gone, he surfaced with a few powerful thrusts of his arms and legs. The drive carried him out of the water, almost to his waist. He filled his lungs and dived deeply again.

There was a feeling of exuberance growing in him now, a sense of having returned at last. The depths of the river, even turbulent and dark, were like home to him. He had been born beside this river. He knew its every mood and feared none of them. He had no need to fear. His strong, deep-chested, thick-waisted body was as buoyant as seasoned wood, the capacity of his lungs was enormous. And he could swim as few men can.

He surfaced again and rode the crest. With no effort at all he floated high, his head and part of his shoulders free. The driving rain, the occasional slap of water that struck his face, did not bother him at all. Nor did the cold. In hours it might numb him dangerously; now he was only a little less than comfortable.

He was free! —that was the thing that mattered. He was safely beyond the reach of any police or prison guard, going where he wanted to go. Downstream, perhaps a hundred miles, was the town of West Mills. He'd lived and worked there. And he'd been tried for murder there, found guilty and sentenced to prison. Since the day they'd taken him from West Mills, handcuffed and shackled, he'd wanted no other thing than to go back.

And now he was going back. The river had done for him what he'd refused to do for himself; it had freed him from prison. As it carried him toward West Mills, it was protecting him with its wide reaches and with the confusion of the disaster it was working. Still more, it was holding in store for him—for the time after West Mills—complete oblivion.

Who could say Donavan had not died in the flood? And who could say, after the flood had gone, that Donavan did not lie buried in the muck and silt, along with a hundred others? All he had to do was manage the business in West Mills carefully, and after it walk carefully through the confusion and out of the confusion to a distant place, a new identity and a free life.

West Mills was the danger point. Donavan had a piece of work to do there, an execution. Jack Murphy, with the black heart and the bloody hands, lived in

West Mills. Murphy was running out of time, though he didn't know it yet. Killing him would not be easy, but the means would somehow be found. For the moment, Donavan put all thought of the future aside. Freedom was a wonderfully heady wine.

For the first time in six years he was alone. No grating laughter reached his ears, no angry cursing, no senseless talk, no yelling in the night. No fawning hand could touch his sleeve indecently. No stink of caged and unwashed bodies could burn his nostrils. There was space around him. There was the sharp biting of fresh, cold water against his hide. There was clean, wet air to fill his lungs. And above him there was no roof of concrete and steel, there was only the open sky.

Donavan was free, and he laughed at that, full-throated laughter he hadn't known in years. He dived again, going deep, then drove himself up to break the surface in a porpoise roll and dived again. He swam far beneath the surface, adding his speed to the swift current, following its twisting, unseen pathways, recoiling as it recoiled, then going up with the sudden rush of it to break the surface in the center of a wide upheaval. A free man ... by the living God and all the saints men pray to ... at last, a free man!

Of the other convicts, only Rudisill and Wilkes and Peebles were still alive, a half mile ahead of Donavan, east of him. Rudisill and Wilkes could swim a little better than most, and they had managed to sustain themselves. But there was great fear in them. The darkness, the cold, the powerful currents, the undertows, the boiling upheavals, were terrifying beyond anything they'd ever known. Wilkes was the first to succumb to the panic, to begin the wild and senseless struggle that ended his life. Rudisill followed in the same way a few moments later.

But not Peebles. That ugly little man did not frighten.

His small, stringy body was tough-fibered, his will to live was indestructible. He paddled clumsily, but furiously, keeping himself afloat long after bigger men and better swimmers had given up. Peebles would not give up; he would not die. And his endless fighting paid off for him. In time, an uprooted tree came to his hands. He fastened to it like a half-drowned cat.

Riding the tree, exuberance came to him, too. He knew he would live now. And he was free. Being alive and free in a flood so vast would be no bad thing, he knew. A man with a gun, a knife, or even a club and the know-how to use it, couldn't help but score big. Houses would stand vacant. Whole towns would be empty. And almost anyone he met would be carrying what they could of their valuables. It would all be free ... free because the flood would cover whatever he had to do to take it.

Tom Sharkey, the guard, was still alive. A far different man than Peebles, he had much the same inflexible will to stay alive. His fight with the river was a carefully controlled one. He husbanded his strength with a miser's care. He reasoned: Each undertow had to return him to the surface in time; a deep breath would sustain him, if he didn't struggle needlessly; his awkward swimming stroke would support him, if he didn't ask too much of it.

But there was nothing like exuberance in him. There was only a grim determination to stay alive somehow. To stay alive, because Tom Sharkey, sergeant, the guard who'd never lost a man, had lost twelve men at one stroke. It didn't matter to him that the fault was not his. They had been his prisoners and prisoners had to serve their time. Some of the twelve had died, he knew. But if he lived, some of the twelve would live with him. And those who lived had to go—would go—back to prison.

Sharkey, Peebles and Donavan were widely

separated. But they had entered the water at the same point. They were being carried by the same currents. Because the currents were treating each man alike, they were going, unknown to each other, toward the same general destination.

The currents carried Donavan away from the normal channel of the river. He knew that, feeling the push of the river slacken as it would upon spreading out across submerged flatlands. Then he began to encounter still-standing trees in the darkness, brush that spoke of fence rows. Still he made no effort to choose a course and stay on it. In this darkness, one was as good as another so long as the general direction was toward the south.

He came upon the north-south highway in a little while. His first hint of it was the bite of barbed wire, the roadside fence, against his legs. He got over it, into the deeper water of the roadside ditch, then felt the graveled shoulder beneath his feet. He waded to the pavement and found the water flowing there only a little more than knee deep.

He waded south along the highway. There was no stretch of it above water, and on the average it ranged from depths above his knees to above his waist. He found three cars stalled in a group, seeing the faint gleam of chrome only a moment before his hands touched it. The owners were gone. Two more empty cars were farther on, then a quarter of a mile of empty road. The water hit him at the waist until a slight rise in the pavement shallowed it a little. He was resting here when he heard Elizabeth Matthews' call.

The sound was faint in the drumming rain, dreary and forlorn, as any imitation of a foghorn must be, but unmistakably human and female. Donavan did not go toward the sound at once. He couldn't bring himself to. Whoever was calling would need help; he swore at that. He hadn't time to help anyone. He couldn't safely help anyone. Worse—this was a bitter discovery to him—he had no desire to help. Why should he help one of the people who had kept him caged the past six years? Why should he help anyone at all?

He fought with himself and lost. He waded on, his anger and his disappointment an ugly taste in his mouth. When he was near enough he called, "Hello ... hello there."

Elizabeth answered at once. "Hello! Hello!" There was doubt in her voice, fear that her ears had tricked her. He called again and Elizabeth knew a gladness and a relief that made her almost senseless. "Yes ... yes, I'm here! Oh, thank God. Help me, help me ... I'd given up hope. I—"

"Steady," Donavan said. "I'll be right with you."

The pavement sloped into a downgrade, the water deepened again and the current began tugging at his legs. Her voice guided him to the car, and he stood beside it, waist-deep in the boil on the downstream side. He couldn't see her in the rain and the darkness, nor could she see him.

"Are you alone?" she asked.

"Alone," he said. "Walking and swimming. Well, you'd better come down. You can't stay up there."

"But the water's deep. The current—"

"Deep and getting deeper," Donavan said quietly. "The dikes have given way upstream. It's taking a while to cover the flatlands, but they'll be covered by ten feet or more. You'll have to get into the water. It might as well be now."

"No ... I can't!"

Donavan moved close to the car. Reaching up, fumbling in the darkness, his big hand found a slim ankle, closed. Elizabeth screamed. He pulled and she came tumbling, screaming, down on top of him. He caught her weight on his shoulder. She fought him wildly, but he forced her legs down into the cold water between himself and the car, to her knees, her thighs, her waist, until her feet were on the pavement. The shock of the chill water stopped her outcries. She could only gasp.

"You'll be all right," he told her. "The water's cold, but you'll get used to it. Now stop fighting. Stop fighting the water and stop fighting me. Get hold of yourself—you can't stay alive if you don't."

Her arms were tight around his neck. She was clinging to him desperately, pressed hard against his naked chest. Now, as the first shock passed, she found that nothing harmful had happened and began to think again. The quiet voice of the man who held her was completely unafraid, completely confident ... his chest was big, his shoulders and arms were very strong. Her courage came back to her.

"I—I lost my head ..."

"It's all right," he said. "And you're going to be all right. But you've got to trust me and do what I say to do. We can't stay here. The water's rising. We'll have to swim."

"The highway—can't we walk?"

"All of the highway is under," he said. "It will be deep under soon. And we can't waste our strength fighting the river. We can only win if we let it carry us along." He brought his face close to hers, trying to see something of it. He could see only a pale, indefinite outline. "It will help if I know a little something about you," he said. "How old are you?"

"Twenty-three."

"Are you in good health? Are you strong?"

"Yes."

"Can you swim?"

"Not in this!"

"But you can swim a hundred yards or so? And you're not afraid, deathly afraid of the water?"

"I'm not that afraid. I can swim and dive as well as most women, I guess. But I'm not a champion."

"You don't need to be," Donavan said. "I'm champion

enough for both of us. That's a truth. Believe it, so you won't panic. I can swim twenty miles without leaving the water. I have, more than once. When we leave here, we'll let this current take us wherever it will until we find shelter of some kind."

"What can we find in this dark?"

"Perhaps nothing," he said. "Then we'll go on until daylight. Hold still now." He ran his hands over her shoulder, down her waist, over her hips and down to her feet. "You'll have to get out of some of those clothes. Your coat, your dress, your girdle, shoes and stockings. Save your slip, if you have to, but we'll tie it around your waist. And save me your coat belt."

She was silent, unmoving.

He said, "Your modesty speaks well for you, but your judgment is faulty. Wet clothes won't keep you warm. Wet, they'll pull you down, tangle your arms and legs and catch on things." He waited a moment. Then he said, "Your modesty may kill you, half-naked you're sure to live—it's your choice."

"Here's my coat belt," she said.

He held the belt of her raincoat in his teeth. He helped her remove her coat. As she lifted her dress and slip, he stripped them off her, over her head. He made the slip into a rope and tied it around her waist. In the turbulence, her wet girdle proved more than she could manage alone; he helped her with that, and with her shoes and stockings.

"Now give me your wrist," he said.

He tied one end of her raincoat belt securely to her wrist. Then he fashioned a loop in the other end, ran it above the biceps of his right arm, drew it tight.

"It's not a towrope," he said. "It's to keep me from losing you in the dark. You'll ride with your hands on my shoulders. Let me do the swimming. Float as shallowly as you can straight behind me; I'll take the worst of the brush and the fences. All right?"

"I'll try."

"Good girl. Now let's be on our way."

He took her hand in his and drew her away from the sheltering eddy beside the car, toward the roadside ditch. She felt him dropping into deeper water, felt the stronger currents dragging at her legs, and fear caught her again.

"Can't we stay on the highway? Please!"

"No ..." He was chest deep, fighting the current. "I know this road and this country. There's no high ground. The water will drive us from the road, and I'd rather leave it where there's a channel cut. The deep water is the safest."

He pulled her hand. She had no choice but to go with him into the deeper water. She gasped as the coldness of it covered her entire body and began swimming, reaching for him. He turned in her clutching arms, guided her hands to his shoulders. He shoved off, riding high to clear the roadside fence, and let the current take them where it would.

After the first moments of terror and uncertainty, Elizabeth was able to control her fear again. No fear was communicated to her from the man beneath her hands. He was able to keep them both afloat with only the smallest movements, and when there was need for swimming, his powerful breaststroke carried them in almost any direction he chose.

This was still the greatest hardship she'd ever known. While she became used to the cold to some degree, it was never less than just bearable, and, as time went on, it seemed to penetrate to her bones. They rode torrents that were almost cataracts, dipping and rising on rolling waves. Spouts of water struck her face endlessly, choking her. They wheeled through eddies, scraped against brush and newly torn-out banks, and were battered by unseen floating debris.

Occasionally the water became still, shallowing to hip deep and knee deep, and they waded. The rain beating on her naked shoulders seemed to warm her, and the return to the cold of the deep water was greater torment. There were a few small areas of ground above water. When they stumbled on one of these, Donavan would let her rest a little, but no matter how hard she protested, he would never let her stay.

"You can't stay," he told her, his voice quiet, impersonal and patient. "This ground will be under in a little while. But even if it weren't going to be, we'd have to go on until we found dry shelter for you. You can't take this cold for long. Too much exposure will kill you. We'll find something soon."

He had to drag her by force from that high ground. On the next, he heard a sound that gave her new strength. "Hear it, girl?" he asked. "That's cattle bawling. We're on or near a farm. There must be buildings ... a barn, a house, a shed."

They went on, wading. The water was quiet, no deeper than their hips, and the land was level. But it had been a grain field, well grown before the flood had come, and the grasslike stalks, standing loose and free under the water, caught at their bare feet and legs like thousands of tentacles. Each stride was enormously difficult. The last of Elizabeth's strength was drained from her. She fell, got up and went on and fell again, and got up and fell and couldn't get up. Donavan took her in his arms and carried her.

A fence ended that field. Beyond it, uneven mud beneath his feet told him he was in a lane much used by livestock. He paused a moment, listening to the still distant bawling of the cattle, thinking. Then he followed the lane in a direction away from the sound of the cattle. In a little more than a hundred yards, he came to a wide, wooden gate, a barnyard gate, standing open. He crossed the barnyard to another fence and followed the fence to another gate. This gate was closed, but easily opened, and there was a brick path that led to a house. Donavan climbed two steps to a porch that was knee-deep under the water. He put Elizabeth on her feet and held her.

"Are you all right?" he said. "Can you stand alone?"

"I—I think so ... yes. Where are we?"

"We've found a house."

"But there's no light."

"No power," Donavan said. "And we can hope the owners got away ahead of the flood. The water's a foot deep over the floor now and climbing." He took the loop of the raincoat belt from his arm. "I'll see what we've got here."

They had a farmhouse, old and not very large. A kitchen—they entered through the back door—a dining room, a living room and an old-fashioned parlor. These things Donavan discovered, wading and groping through the darkness, running his hands over furniture that still stood on the floors.

"We're in luck," he said. "I can't find a bedroom on this floor. That means we've got two floors with bedrooms above. Stand fast until I find the stairs."

Elizabeth waited in the darkness by the kitchen doorway. She was sagging with exhaustion, but far worse was the cold. Now it had penetrated to every part of her. Her jaws were chattering, her body ached, her mind was sick and numb. She heard Donavan say he'd found the stairs, but she couldn't answer or go to him. He came to her. The first touch of his hands on her flesh told him what the trouble was. He lifted her in his arms and carried her. He found a bedroom upstairs and a bed with coverings. He stood her beside it.

"Strip," he said. "Strip to the buff and wait. I'll go look for towels."

She was stripped and in bed, shivering miserably and sick beyond caring, when he returned. His groping hands found her. "I told you to wait," he said, without anger. "But it's all right. There's another bed." The blankets and sheet were pulled from her, a thick bath towel dropped across her breasts. Another towel, enclosing his big hands, began to rub her feet and legs. His hands were rough, vigorous and insistent, but somehow they didn't hurt her. And they didn't stop with her feet and legs. They went on, impersonally, until they had brought warmth and circulation to every part of her body. He swung her feet to the floor, then, found her wrist and drew her up.

"Come on ... into a dry bed." He led her to another bedroom and another bed. He held the covers open for her, guided her under them and tucked her in. "I'll see if I can find pajamas or a nightgown." He went away and came back. "No luck. You'll have to make do. Would another blanket help?"

"I'll be all right."

"Good girl. If you begin to chill again, call me. I think we can beat it with massage. At least, we can try."

She was silent for a moment. Then: "I wish I could see you."

"Why?"

"So I could thank you," she said. "I can't thank just a voice in the dark for what you've done. Give me your hand." Her hand found his and she gripped it. "Thanks ... so much."

"I deserve no thanks," he said. "None at all." She heard him turn away. "Rest now ... sleep. I'll be near."

CHAPTER TWO

Elizabeth went to sleep in darkness, in a room filled with the sound of drumming rain. She awakened sometime after daylight to find the room almost still. The rain had stopped. The bawling of cattle was a distant sound, the voice of the flood was muted. She was tired, drowsy and warm. The weight of the blankets told her that another had been added during the night, and that realization brought others, awakening her fully. She sat up, holding the covers about her shoulders.

She was alone in the room. The door was closed. Her underthings were draped over the rail at the foot of the bed. Besides, there were a faded pair of jeans, torn but serviceable, and a faded sweat shirt. A worn pair of tennis shoes was on the floor beside the bed. She got up and dressed hurriedly. The nylon underthings were dry, the jeans and sweat shirt were too small for her, the shoes were much too big.

"He was a growing boy," she said. "All hands and feet."

Elizabeth was tall, slim almost to the point of being angular, but well formed. Her legs were long, her hips were compact and her breasts were small and round and firm. There was angularity in her face, too, a minimum of flesh molded over good bone structure. Her eyes were gray and large; her mouth was wide, the sloping line of it clean and honest. She was not a pretty girl; her rangy figure, the strong proportions of her features prevented that. But she had the beauty of a well-bred girl, carefully and gently raised.

She found a comb on the dresser and brought order to short-cut, ash-blond hair. Then she opened the bedroom door and called. There was no answer. She moved into the narrow hallway and called again. Still no answer. A door across the hall was open, the bedroom beyond it was empty.

"He didn't leave me!" she said. "He couldn't!"

She called again, loudly. No answer. Standing silently, she could hear only the weary bawling of the cattle, the creaking of the old house, the quiet voice of the flood. She couldn't doubt that she was alone in the house. She ran to the head of the stairs. The steps went down and disappeared into water, a floating table was canted and jammed in the lower hallway. She ran to the window at the rear end of the hall.

"Dear God ..."

The clouds had broken, there were patches of blue

sky and warm sunlight, but ugly, muddy, wind-scuffed water had covered the land. She could see only an occasional tree and a few rafts of brush and wreckage. She found the window latch and lifted the window. The depth of the water was clearly marked on the wall of the house; the windows of the floor below were half submerged. She remembered the water had been only knee-deep in those rooms the night before. During the night, then, the water had risen three feet, perhaps four.

Leaning far out, she looked toward the main channel of the river. She could not distinguish it. With the exception of a few small islands of high ground, a few houses standing with porch roofs awash, a drunken line of telephone poles that marked the submerged north-south highway, the flood had covered everything. There was no movement anywhere, human or animal. And fear leaped in her breast like a live thing—in all this she was alone!

She turned from the window and ran to the window at the opposite end of the hall. She broke fingernails on the latch, she tore her hands getting the window up. Again she leaned far out ... and almost wept with relief at what she saw.

The flood was not all prevailing. There was land and life in this direction. A small herd of white-faced cattle was huddled on a bit of an island, bawling forlornly. A quarter of a mile distant a hogback of land, three feet above water, ran like a dike to the north; beyond that, across more water, was the dark rise of endless high ground. Close at hand, there was a wooded lot where huge oak trees were standing in quiet water, and closer still were the barn and two out-buildings, still on their foundations.

But she was alone, and because of that, her fear did not leave her until she saw Donavan again. She knew at once he was the man who had helped her the night before; he was helping another man in the same way.

They came into view from beyond the wall of the barn, Donavan first, swimming an easy, powerful breaststroke, the other man floating behind, his hands on Donavan's shoulders.

There was no walking for them, no wading, as there had been the night before. Now Donavan had to swim every foot of the way between barn and house. Elizabeth turned from the window when they reached the back porch. She went to the stairway. The deep, quiet voice that had spoken to her in the darkness the night before was speaking again.

"Can you stand up, Peebles? Can you walk? All right, through there, to the left, you'll find the stairs. There are two bedrooms on the floor above. The girl is sleeping in the one on the right. Take the other one. Get dried off, get in bed. I'll be back."

"Don't be a damn fool!" Peebles said. His was a thin voice, choked and shaking with exhaustion and cold, but it was full of snarling protest. "Leave 'im there!"

There was no answer.

"Good God, man!" the snarling voice said. "What's he to you? Leave 'im there! Let him find his own way outa this mess. Or let him go to hell! Listen to me, Donavan! I—"

The voice broke off with a curse. Elizabeth heard the man raging to himself as he splashed his way toward the stairs. She ran to the hall window again. Donavan was swimming away from the house toward the wooded lot. She called to him. He stopped, turned and looked up at her, treading water.

"You all right?" he asked.

"Yes … are you coming back?"

"In a little while. There's a man hung up in an oak out there. I'm going out to bring him in."

"Be careful!"

"Always careful," he said.

He rolled and went on again, his arms moving in a long overhand stroke that left a steady wake behind him. Elizabeth turned from the window. The newcomer, Peebles, was crawling up the stairs, panting and cursing. Afraid of a man who cursed like that, Elizabeth backed away. Peebles reached the upper floor, fell sprawling, then clawed his way up to stand erect.

Elizabeth saw a thin man, almost scrawny, shaking and miserable with the cold. His only covering was trousers torn off raggedly at the knees. She could see the rib cage of his narrow chest plainly through the water-welted skin, she could see stringy, wirelike muscles in his arms and legs. He took a pair of steel-rimmed spectacles from a pocket, put them on and stared at Elizabeth with round and angry eyes.

"You're the girl, eh?" His voice was a rasping snarl, made bitter by the sickness in him. "Don't stand there! Can't you see I'm half dead? Show me the bedroom! Get me some towels or something to dry me off!" He waited a moment, staring. "What do I have to do, beg you? Get going!"

Elizabeth ran past him to the bedroom across the hall from the one she'd used. The towels were there, spread to dry. She caught them up and threw them at the little man as he lurched in through the doorway. Then she ran to her bedroom and closed the door. Small and scrawny this Peebles might be, but no one could mistake the strength in him, or the evilness of his mind. Elizabeth sat on the edge of a chair, holding herself in tight-clasped arms. The bed in the other room creaked under the small man's weight. There was muttered cursing, then silence. When the silence had gone unbroken for fifteen minutes, Elizabeth opened the door softly and went to the hall window again.

Her gray eyes were wide and very sober as they looked out over the flood. Hers was a swift mind, sensitive and far-reaching, and no single aspect of her position here could escape her. She was not safe from the flood yet, by any means. No one could be called safe until they were far away from the river. She was not away from it; she was right in the middle of it. And she couldn't get out of it alone. Someone had to help her—this man Donavan, probably, because no one else was near. He could help her, or not help her, just as he chose, and that was too much power for a woman to give any man.

She had to face the fact that she was female. How could she forget it with a man as ugly as that Peebles around? If she had to depend on him to help her ... brother! But even so, a female caught in this mess with any two strange men—three, if Donavan brought in another—was in no happy predicament. You could say no, you could threaten and scream and cry, but what else? Nothing else. They could do whatever they wanted to, then drop you in the river afterward.

Elizabeth made a face, suddenly angry with herself. This was a stupid, morbid, scare-baby way of thinking. It reminded her of a piece of her mother's scolding: "Liz, it's time you grew up. All men don't have hooves and horns. Once in a while you meet a decent one. But you're not going to meet a decent one, hiding down there in college, taking post-graduate work year after year. And you are hiding—deny it till you're blue in the face, and I'll say so. I say you're training for a career as a frightened old maid!"

There wasn't a word of truth in it, of course. Her way of life—she'd explained it carefully many times—was a matter of personal preference, decided upon by a careful weighing of the merits of other ways. Fear, or dislike of men, had no part of it. The quiet secluded life appealed to her, and what was wrong with that? Did every woman need a husband and a family of six children?

Aloud, Elizabeth said, "Well! If mother could see me now! One man ... I'm going to be surrounded by men!"

And she decided that if it had been at all possible, this was just the kind of skulduggery her mother would work. She'd decided a year or two ago that her daughter had been loved and coddled too much. No guts, was the vulgar way she'd put it. Marooned with three men would be just exactly the trial-by-fire, sink-or-swim sort of thing her mother would come up with. And if she'd been able to whisper into the ear of destiny, it was a sure thing she had.

There was the sound of bare feet thumping the floor in the bedroom behind her. "Hey!" Peebles called. "Hey, you, out there! Get me another blanket!"

Without turning, Elizabeth said, "The blankets are in the room across the hall from you."

She stood motionless at the window, arms crossed, face quietly furious. She was not going to let herself be ordered about by a man like Peebles. She heard the bedroom door open behind her.

"What's the matter? You too proud to help a guy?"

Elizabeth said, "I'll answer to a request, not an order."

"Well ..." Peebles said. "So we got a real snooty dame, have we? Ain't that something. You wait till I get on my feet, sister, and we'll see about this."

Elizabeth pressed her lips tight. She heard the bare feet go into the bedroom she'd used, heard them return to the other bedroom and the door slam. "Beast!" she whispered. It had a brave, defiant sound, but she didn't fool herself with it. Her knees were shaking and she couldn't argue with them. She was scared. If this Donavan turned out to be even a little bit like Peebles, she was a gone goose. "You got your wish," she whispered to her mother. "There are no ivy-covered walls around here to hide behind."

Now she saw Donavan come into view again. He was bringing another man to safety, but not in the same fashion he'd brought the other. This one was too far gone to hold to Donavan's shoulders. Donavan was swimming a sidestroke, his right arm across the upturned chest of the man. It was slow, hard work, but Donavan came steadily on. Elizabeth was waiting for him where the stairs met the water.

"Can I help you?"

"I'll make it all right."

Donavan pushed the floating table out of the stair doorway and came into the stairwell, backing onto the stairs, waist deep. The man he'd brought was floating on his back. Donavan flipped him over, face down, ducked under him and came up with the man on his shoulders.

"Out of the way," he said to Elizabeth. "I've got him."

Elizabeth hurried up the stairs and stood aside. Donavan was breathing heavily and lurching beneath the weight, but he needed no help. He carried the man to the bedroom Elizabeth had used and eased him to the floor beside the bed.

"Still with me, Tom?" he asked.

The man's eyes opened. He didn't speak; he couldn't. Elizabeth, standing in the doorway, knew how sick the man was. His long, bony body was shaking uncontrollably. His lean face was painfully drawn, his lips were blue with cold, white-rimmed. He was bald and that, aging him, seemed to add immeasurably to his suffering. Elizabeth turned away hurriedly as Donavan bent to strip the trousers from the prostrate man, and in a moment she was back with towels.

"Only one is dry," she said.

"One will have to do," Donavan said. "But save it to rub him down. Dry him with the damp ones." He wrung out the man's soaked trousers and hung them on a chair. "And don't be gentle with him. You have to get rough to get his blood moving again. Then get him into bed."

Elizabeth's eyes went wide. "I ..."

He looked at her. "Why not you?"

Now she saw him clearly for the first time. She saw a big man. He was not beautifully sculptured; he was strong, thick of waist and chest and shoulder. He wore only cut-off trousers, and the skin above and below was hairless and only faintly marked by the water and the cold. His head was round, the short hair of it was plastered to his forehead in a straight line above his brows. His dark eyes were quiet, level and direct. They looked at her without favor or disfavor—impersonally, as if she were nothing much at all.

Her face flamed. "Do you realize what you're asking?"

"Yes," Donavan said. "This man needs your help. Just as you needed my help last night. I'm asking you to give him the same help I gave you."

"But he's a man!"

"Obviously," Donavan said.

There was panic in Elizabeth. Donavan didn't consider the task at all unreasonable and to refuse was not going to make a close friend of him. But she had to refuse. She'd never seen a naked man in her life, much less touched one. Now a burning shame was added to all the rest. She couldn't meet the level stare of Donavan's eyes. She turned away and fled into the hall.

Donavan didn't call her back. He looked after her a moment without a change in expression. Then he picked up the towels. He dried Tom Sharkey and helped him into the bed. There he used the single dry towel to rub warmth and life back into the thin man's aching limbs. When he put Sharkey under the bed covering, everything that could be done for the man had been done. He went into the hall. Elizabeth was standing at the window. She heard him but she did not turn. He didn't speak to her. He went down the stairs and waded into the water on the floor below.

When he came to the upper floor again, his arms were loaded with things he'd found—a short-handled ax, a kitchen carving knife, a five-gallon can, matches and paper. He took them into the room where the small man lay and dropped them on the floor.

"Peebles," he said. "Get up, get dressed."

"Man, I can't. I'm half dead!"

He remained in bed, tightly wrapped in blankets, watching Donavan. Donavan used the ax on a chair, smashing it to kindling. He knocked out the window-frame, glass and wood, and then set the five-gallon can close by it. There was mud in the bottom of the can for insulation. He chopped a hole for a draft. Then with the kindling, paper and matches, he built a fire. He watched the smoke lift to the high ceiling and cover the ceiling and then begin to drift out of the broken window. Donavan turned to Peebles again.

"Get up," he said quietly.

"What's the rush? After all I been through, I—"

Donavan moved with a suddenness amazing for his bulk. He tore away the blankets that covered Peebles. A big hand closed on one of Peebles' ankles. Donavan set his feet and heaved, and Peebles was dragged from the bed. The swing of Donavan's big shoulders sent Peebles sliding across the floor to crash against the wall. Peebles' head struck hard. The small man yelled with pain and held his head and cursed. But he did not curse Donavan. He had known the big man too long to risk that. He fought back his anger and got up to put on his wet, cut-off trousers, setting his teeth against the cold. He went to the make-shift stove to absorb some of the first heat. Since anger was dangerous, he tried a friendliness that was not quite fawning.

"How do you do it?" he said. "The whole world's under water and you come up with dry matches?"

"Thank some child for that," Donavan said. "The matches were on a high shelf out of a child's reach."

"Find any cigarettes?"

"No. But there's a safety razor and some blades."

"What do I need a shave for? That babe? I asked her to get me a blanket—she tell you? She told me to go jump. For that one, I'll let my beard grow. I'll whisker her good."

"I wouldn't try, if I were you." Donavan used the ax

on a chest of drawers and built a supply of fuel. "There's canned food in the pantry below. And kettles and pans. Get up whatever you think we need to put together a meal."

"Where're you going?"

"After meat."

"Say ..." Peebles' narrow face twisted in a grin. "Man, you got something there. One o' them steers, eh? After the slum they been feedin' us, how'll a chunk of good, red meat go? I could eat half a steer myself!"

Donavan took the ax and the knife and went into the hall again. Elizabeth was still at the window, but she had turned. With time to think, the wisdom of making amends to the big man had become very clear to her. She was ready with an apology. "I know it must seem silly to you, but really it was asking too much. Of me, anyway. You see, I—"

Donavan was not listening to her. His quiet eyes were making a careful inspection. He saw the good bones in her face and the sensitive line of her mouth. There could be no mistaking the kind of girl she was, the kind of family she'd come from, or the life she'd lived. A good girl, badly spoiled, probably, but virtuous. Her family had money, if not a lot, at least more than enough. And she was surely a stranger to roughnecks. She was out of place here. As out of place here, as that slim body was out of place in a boy's sweatshirt and jeans. The fit was very tight. Where the garments failed to meet, he could see the nylon of her underthings and patches of bare flesh.

"Is it necessary to stare at me?" she asked. Her face was white again, her lips were tight.

"Just curious," he said. He turned away and went into the other bedroom. There by the bed, he looked down at Tom Sharkey. "You're a tough one," he said. "You'll make it."

"I'll make it, thanks to you." Sharkey's voice was hardly more than a whisper, but there was strength in his pale blue eyes again. "I've been layin' here tryin' to figure out why you did it."

"There was no reason not to."

"Plenty of reason, and you damned well know it. If you'd stayed out of sight for a few months, who could have sworn you were still alive? They'd have ended up calling you dead and buried in the muck somewhere. But now I know you're alive. And now I've got to take you back."

"I'm never going back, Tom."

"D'you think savin' my life could make a difference? I took an oath when I took that job, Donavan. I meant what I said. And I mean to live up to it."

"I know you do, Tom."

"And you're my prisoner. You're going back."

"I'm never going back, Tom."

Color began to burn in Sharkey's lean face. He stared long and hard at Donavan's quiet eyes. "Then you'd better kill me now," he whispered hoarsely. "Because if I live I'll take you back. That's a promise. I'll take you back, if I have to kill you to get you there!"

Donavan nodded. "It's your job to try."

The things they'd said had brought Elizabeth to the doorway. She was standing there now, shocked, unable to believe the things she'd heard. She could only stare at them. And Peebles, too, had heard the conversation. He came from the other bedroom to push Elizabeth aside. His hair was awry, his eyes were angry behind his steel-rimmed glasses. He crossed to the bed and looked down at Tom Sharkey. Then he looked at Donavan.

"What'd I tell you?" he asked. "All you're gonna get for savin' this dirty screw's neck is trouble! You could've let him go to hell; he was halfway there. But no, you got to bring him in. So you see what happens. You couldn't expect a louse like this to show you any gratitude. He ain't got it in him!"

Elizabeth said, "What are you saying? What is—"

Peebles said, "Shut up!"

Donavan said nothing.

Sharkey, his pale eyes fixed on Peebles now, said, "It doesn't matter what Donavan did for me. I'm only a guard. What matters is what you two did. You were both tried and fairly convicted—Donavan for murder, you for armed robbery. You've got a lot of time to—"

"Oh, no!" Elizabeth said.

Peebles jumped as if he'd been stung. He whirled. "Will you get out of here?" he rasped. "Go on, beat it!" And when she only stared at him with wide eyes, he said, "Donavan, tell her to take a walk for herself."

Donavan looked at her briefly. "She'll hear it sooner or later. She may as well hear it now."

Sharkey said, "You both have got a lot of time left to serve. And it's my job to see that you serve it. You're my prisoners now. Get it through your heads. You're going back."

"Will you get this guy?" Peebles said. "He's flat on his back and shootin' off his mouth like he was nine feet tall and had a rifle in both hands! Why, you—" he reached down suddenly and closed a hand on Sharkey's face, his fingers biting deep. "Who the hell do you think you're talkin' to? A couple o' chumps?"

Sharkey didn't try to answer, didn't try to escape the hand that held his face. He only stared at Peebles, his pale blue eyes unwavering, relentless and cold.

"Let me tell you something, screw," Peebles said. "We're outa the joint, and we like being out. We're not goin' back. Before you make a pass at tryin' to take us, you'd better look around. Where's your rifle? Where's your help? You haven't got 'em, have you? There's just you, and us. And another thing—what's it going to cost us if we knock you off? You'd be just another stiff floating down the river." His fingers sank deeper into the flesh of Sharkey's face. "Y'better think it over, screw," he said. "Think it over twice!"

Sharkey only stared at him.

Elizabeth said, "Let go of him! You're hurting him!"

"And that ain't all I'm goin' to do," Peebles said.

Elizabeth's mind was running wild. She was frantically trying to make sense of what she'd heard, and just as frantically trying to deny she'd heard it. A murderer ... this Donavan was a murderer? And Peebles an armed robber. And Sharkey was a policeman, or something? It couldn't be! It couldn't happen to her. She couldn't believe it. But she had to believe Peebles' fingers digging into Sharkey's face. That was happening now, before her eyes.

"Make him stop," she said to Donavan.

"It's not my fight," Donavan said. He went past her to the doorway, turned there. "Peebles will get food up from below," he said. "I'm going after meat. If you'd like to eat with us, it might be a good idea to see what you can do about getting a meal started." He turned away.

"Wait!" Elizabeth said.

He didn't wait. He went into the hall toward the stairs. And Elizabeth ran after him. She caught his arm and stopped him. Her face was twisted, her voice was furious.

"Come back and make him stop, do you hear?"

Donavan looked at her quietly. "Why should I?"

"You heard what he said! He might kill the man!"

"I don't think so," Donavan said. "Not for a while, anyway. Peebles needs time to get himself worked up. But in any case, as I told you, it's not my fight. Peebles is a convict, Tom Sharkey is a guard. They can do their own fighting. I won't take sides."

"But you've got to! Sharkey is sick."

"Then he shouldn't get tough with Peebles."

"But Sharkey is a guard."

"And Peebles is a convict, like myself. It happens that I owe him no more than I owe Tom Sharkey."

With that, he turned and went down the stairs. Elizabeth watched him wade into water that reached his chest. He held the knife in one hand, the ax in the other. She wanted to shriek at him. But she couldn't, her throat was suddenly locked tight. In his quiet way, he was worse than Peebles. He was ruthless! Even now, he was going out with an ax and a knife to kill a helpless animal—somehow, in her mind, that added up to an enormous thing. She stood at the head of the stairs, a hand at her throat, horrified. The water splashed and became quiet. Donavan had gone away. Now she could hear Peebles' voice grating in the room behind her. There was a moment of silence, then the hard, slapping sound of a hand striking flesh.

Elizabeth's legs almost gave way. "Oh, no!"

Peebles came into the hall and saw her standing against the wall. Peebles had changed oddly. In spite of his small, bony legs and his ridiculous, cut-off trousers, he was strutting. His narrow shoulders were back, his thin chest out-thrust, his stringy arms were held away from his sides, bent at the elbows. Even his voice held a swagger.

"Hey, you!" he said to Elizabeth. "Come here!"

When she didn't respond, he came to her, caught her by an arm and spun her away from the wall. There was fear in her and loathing, but she did not shrink away. The defiance, if it could be called defiance, brought a twisted grin to Peebles' face, a new interest to his eyes.

"Well, well," he said. "Who d'you think you're kiddin'? You're about as tough as a bottle of cream, and don't you think I don't know it. Come on, now, straighten up. Give us a good look at you." She didn't straighten up, but he made his long inspection, missing no part of her face or figure, no tear or gap in her jeans and sweatshirt. "Not bad," he said. "A little skinny for my taste, but not bad at all. I got to hand it to that Donavan. Six years in the joint, and the first night out he finds himself a woman. First things first, I always say. How come he run into you?"

"It's none of your business," Elizabeth said.

"So?" Peebles grinned again. "Well, maybe it ain't, since Donavan saw you first. But let me tell you something, chick. You won't have to look far when Donavan gets done with you to find another man. What do you think of that?" He came toward her, still grinning.

"Don't touch me!" Elizabeth cried.

"Who's goin' to?" he said.

But he tried to pinch her as he went by, and when she escaped him he only laughed. He went down the stairs. Elizabeth listened to his clumsy splashing on the floor below; then, hearing Sharkey moving about in the bedroom, she ran to him. He was a prison guard—in a sense, the police. He had put on his trousers and was wearing a blanket around his lean shoulders. He was a married man with two young daughters of his own; he knew well what the fear in the girl was. He was kind and sympathetic which may not have been wise. She reacted to it by collapsing on the edge of the bed, sobbing uncontrollably. He sat beside her, an arm around her shoulders until the sobbing stopped. Then she wiped her eyes with the heel of either hand.

"Is—is he really a murderer?"

"He's really a murderer." Sharkey could see no point in hiding the truth; the truth might better equip her. "He was serving a life sentence in the state prison. He was one of a crew of twelve I had trying to save the Humboldt dike. We were cut off and washed out. The flood killed most of the men, I guess. The bodies of two were washed into the grove of oaks with me. It set Donavan and Peebles free."

They were silent, hearing Peebles in the hall again. He came to the doorway, trailing water. He had a kettle full of some home-canned food, a frying pan and a heavy, narrow-bladed boning knife thrust into his belt. He showed them his twisted grin. "Don't get cozy with that girl," he said to Sharkey. "Donavan saw her first." He left the food and implements in the other bedroom and went to the floor below again.

"He's horrible," Elizabeth said.

"A bad one," Sharkey agreed. "He was serving a term for armed robbery, but he's a lot worse than that. A rotten soul, rotten clear through. Don't turn your back on him. Don't be caught alone with him."

"Oh, Lord!" Elizabeth said. "What are we going to do."

Sharkey's lean face was sober, his eyes had turned cold again. "I'm going to see them both back in prison. Or dead. I'll do what I can for you. I don't know what it will be, but I'll try, you can be sure of that."

"If you fight with them, they'll kill you!"

"I'm not an easy man to kill."

"Do you have to take them back ... to prison, I mean?"

"It's my job."

"I know that. But it's senseless to try. There are two of them against you. Couldn't you say you'd changed your mind, even if you really hadn't?"

"That kind of a lie would be a waste of breath," Sharkey said. "They know me better. They know I'll never give an inch to them; they know I'll go straight ahead. And it's not as bad as it looks. I'm almost myself again, and when I'm myself, I can handle Peebles in any kind of a fight."

"But Donavan?"

"Donavan could break me in half with his bare hands. But I don't think he will. You don't save a man's life in one hour and kill him in the next. He knew what he'd be up against if he brought me in, but he did it anyway. He's got something else in mind, something besides killing me."

"He'd let Peebles do it," Elizabeth said. "He told me he didn't care what happened to either of you. He said he owed neither of you anything, and he meant it."

"And I told you I can handle Peebles."

Peebles, in the hall again, heard this as Sharkey had meant him to. A second armful of provisions and utensils hit the floor of the hallway, and Peebles came into the room. The heavy, narrow-bladed knife was in his hand. He stopped halfway to Elizabeth and Sharkey, water dripping from his body and his ragged trousers. Behind his steel-rimmed glasses, his eyes held an ugly shine. He pointed the knife at Sharkey's throat.

"Who can handle Peebles?" he asked.

"I can, you dirty little punk," Sharkey said. He didn't move or lift his voice. "And that knife won't help you. Get close to me with it, and I'll shove it down your throat butt first."

"Well, now ..." Peebles said. "Listen to him, will you? He's real tough. Maybe we ought to find out how tough he really is ..." He went into a crouch. With his thin body and his cut-off trousers, he would have looked ridiculous, if it hadn't been for the knife—the knife was lethal. "Yes, sir ..." he said softly. "Let's just see how tough you are ..."

Sharkey's only move was a shrug of his lean shoulders that dropped the blanket from him. He seemed relaxed, his large hands resting easily on his knees. He watched Peebles with unwavering eyes that were like chips of pale blue ice.

"C'mon," Peebles said. "Do I cut you sittin' down?"

"Try to cut me," Sharkey said.

To Elizabeth, this was all impossible, all unreal. It was something from a book, or an ugly nightmare. But there was murder in Peebles' twisted face. And Sharkey's face, in a different way, was just as murderous. They meant what they had said, both of them. They were willing to fight, ready to fight, and one of them would die. And she could only watch with shocked, unthinking disbelief.

"Get up, screw! Get up!"

"Come after me," Sharkey said.

"All right ... I'm comin' ..."

Sharkey said, "Get out of the way, girl."

When she didn't move, he put a hand under her arm, lifting her from the edge of the bed, and shoved her across the room. Elizabeth stumbled and fell. Sharkey did not see her fall. He had not taken his eyes from Peebles. Peebles came forward slowly, flat-footed, waddling a little. The knife was held low, point up, in his right hand; his left hand was to the side and a little above it. Just out of reach of Sharkey, he paused. His body weaving in a half-crouch, he looked for an opening. Sharkey was perfectly still. Peebles feinted a thrust, and still Sharkey didn't move. When the true thrust came, Sharkey twisted his lean body out of the way and the knife blade missed his chest. And Sharkey's counter-move missed—Peebles jerked his wrist out of Sharkey's closing fingers and danced away. Now Sharkey was on his feet.

"This time," Peebles said. "This is the time ..."

"Let's have it," Sharkey said.

Again, Peebles came forward in his weaving half-crouch, again Sharkey waited, poised and motionless. Elizabeth, on her feet now, backed deep into a corner, watched in staring horror. A scream was building in her throat. Peebles feinted again. Sharkey lifted a little on the balls of his feet, but that was all. The second feint was followed by a quick, true thrust aimed at the flat, bare stomach just above Sharkey's belt—impossible to avoid, but Sharkey avoided it. And this time his countermove did not miss. His hand closed on the wrist above the hand that held the knife and locked there.

Elizabeth screamed.

The two men were still for a moment, motionless, straining, the knife high in the air. Then suddenly they exploded in a fury of movement. Peebles was short and thin, but his muscles were wirelike, his wild strength nearly equal to Sharkey's. Sharkey held to

Peebles' wrist as Peebles threw himself wildly about, twisting and kicking and slugging, trying to get free. Sharkey tried to drive home a crippling blow with his free fist, but he could find no target. Both men fell to the floor, got up and fell again. Now, with Elizabeth's screams filling the room, they lay panting and straining, one trying to break the grip, the other to hold it. And Donavan came at this moment and found them thus.

"Belay that!" he shouted.

It was a harsh, deep-chested command. He came through the door in a bull-like rush. He bent and caught Peebles by the hips, lifting him, tearing him loose from Sharkey's grasp. A kick of a bare foot sent Sharkey sprawling, a heave of Donavan's shoulders sent Peebles flying through the bedroom door. The small man struck the wall across the hall and fell, cursing. Sharkey got up slowly, watchfully. But Donavan had no more time for him. Elizabeth was still screaming. He caught her by her upper arms. "Stop it!" he said. "Stop it!" Then he shook her hard until she stopped screaming. He let go of her and she ran to the bed and threw herself upon it, face down. Donavan turned to Sharkey.

"What went on here?"

"Peebles found a knife," Sharkey said. "He decided he'd cut me, or try to. I'm sorry you got back so soon."

"Maybe you're lucky I did," Donavan said.

He went to the bedroom door. Peebles was standing in the hall, still furious, but controlling his fury now. The knife was in his belt, he was rubbing his wrist.

"No more of that," Donavan said. "There's meat at the foot of the stairs. Get it up here."

"The screw asked for it!" Peebles said. "He got—"

"Get the meat," Donavan said. "Now!"

And Peebles obeyed. He was back in a moment, half dragging, half carrying the hind quarter of a steer. Donavan looked into the bedroom and saw Sharkey trying to comfort Elizabeth. Donavan followed Peebles into the other bedroom.

"Build up the fire," he said. "I'll cut the meat."

Donavan and Peebles prepared the meal. Canned corn, canned beans, canned tomatoes and meat ... a huge quantity of meat. The meat was over-fresh and not well-cooked, but there was needed strength and energy in it, and Donavan and Peebles both ate enormously. Elizabeth and Sharkey did not come near them. When Donavan and Peebles had finished, there was still food left. Donavan put it in a large kettle.

"You goin' to feed those two?" Peebles asked.

"That's right," Donavan said.

"You the same as told the girl she couldn't eat if she didn't help," Peebles said. "But go ahead, feed her up—she's your baby. Just lay off that Sharkey. Let 'im starve!"

Donavan stared at him. "Any more advice?"

"Donavan ... for cripe's sake! All I said was—" He broke off, cursing. "All right ... forget it!"

Donavan took the kettle of food into the bedroom across the hall. Sharkey was at the window. He turned. The girl was sitting on the edge of the bed. She had been crying, but she was not crying now. Her face was tear-streaked, but it had firmness. She looked at Donavan, her lips tight.

Donavan said, "What's your name, girl?"

Through tight lips, she said, "Elizabeth Matthews."

"All right, Elizabeth. Here's food for you. It's not too good, but it's hot and it's filling. I want you and Tom to eat. That's an order."

Scornfully, she said, "Are you concerned about us now?"

Donavan looked at her a long moment. "I'm less concerned about you than about myself," he said. "I've got to take care of you for a while yet, and I don't want you to be a burden. I want you strong enough to help. There's still rough going ahead." He turned toward the door.

Elizabeth said, "You'd better be concerned!"

Donavan stopped and came about slowly. His voice was quiet when he said, "Just why had I better be concerned?"

Defiantly, Elizabeth said, "Because if anything happens to either of us, you'll be held responsible. By me, if I'm alive to tell about it, or by my father, if I'm not. It may not impress you, but my family is very well known."

"I'm impressed," Donavan said. "But not greatly. You see almost everything than can be done to me has been done. And in one sense your family had a hand in it. You are among the righteous people who sent me to prison for life."

"You're a murderer," Elizabeth said. "Are we supposed to let murderers run around loose?"

"No, of course not."

"You could be killed—that could still be done."

"True," Donavan said. "But Sharkey's already promised me that. I don't know you or your family very well. But I know Sharkey is a tough one. If I can get past Sharkey, you and your family will be no worry."

Angrily, she said. "What are you going to do with us?"

"You'll see in good time."

"Are you going to give yourself up?"

"Certainly not."

"What are you going to do?"

Soberly, Donavan said, "That's my affair."

He turned and went out of the room. In the other room, Peebles, who'd found a whetstone when he'd found the boning knife, was honing the blade toward a razor edge. Donavan put a pan of water on the still-glowing coals of the crude stove and loaded the safety razor with a fresh blade. Peebles got up and closed the door. Then he took up the knife and whetstone and came to sit against the wall beside Donavan.

"This is just between you an' me," he said. His voice was only a little louder than the soft sound the knife made against the stone. "I heard the babe ask you what you figured on doin'—I mean, after we've got out've here. So I'm goin' to ask the same question. Only it's not to be nosey, see. It's a business proposition. You an' me are in the same fix. It makes sense we team up. We could—"

"I'll go my way alone."

"Wait a minute!" Peebles said. "This is a helluva big flood. Whole towns are gettin' washed out. There's a ton of stuff layin' around, just askin' to be picked up. And there's this—" He held up the knife. "In the right kind of hands, it's as good as a gun. It'll get us a gun. And you're gonna need one. Help, too. I'll give you a hand—"

"You'll give me nothing." Donavan's voice was quiet, but it held a cold edge. "Get it straight. I don't care where you go, or what you do. But where I'm going and what I'm going to do is my business."

Peebles' eyes held an ugly shine. "Won't tell me, eh?"

"I won't tell you."

"Okay," Peebles said. "No hurry. Maybe later."

He went back to whetting the knife. Donavan used the water and the razor and shaved. Then he went to stand before the window that looked out over the flood, upstream of the house. The sky was still broken and where the sun struck there was humid warmth; but there was a black wall of clouds to the north that promised more rain. The level of the flood was still rising. A great volume of water had been needed to cover the flatlands, and there had been a period of slack and slow rise while the river accomplished this. Now the task was nearly completed and the current was returning.

Donavan watched the current work on one of the outbuildings—an equipment shed, or a workshop—pushing at the upstream wall. The shed was trembling, before long it would be gone. The time it stood would depend upon how much flood-borne wreckage came against it. There was a good deal of it in Donavan's view: uprooted trees, scraps of lumber, fence posts, brush, a kitchen chair floating oddly half erect—all moving idly, but steadily downstream. An hour, perhaps two, Donavan thought, and the shed would be gone.

Now his mind turned to the question Elizabeth and Peebles had asked. What was he going to do? It was not a question he would answer for anyone. He would not say, "I'm going to West Mills. And in West Mills I'm going to find a man named Jack Murphy. And this man I'm going to kill ..." No, he would not say it. But he was going to do it—of that, he was irrevocably certain.

West Mills lay something less than a hundred miles downstream. He didn't know how he'd get there; the means would come to hand. But he knew the river well. This house stood a mile or two below the Humboldt dike. Fiddle Island would be a mile or two below this point; the navigation light on the island would be almost under now. Farther south, three tall trees and a silo on the east bank would mark Major Creek. Sand Island would be next, then Half Moon Island, then Lebannon.

Lebannon, just now, would be a town in serious trouble—the dikes gone, the streets flooded, power and telephone poles down. But he had no business in Lebannon. He'd stay far offshore and ride the center of the flood. Past Lemon Island, Johnsonville, Big Molly and Peter's Moorage. In season, in other years, he'd fished the sandbars off Peter's Moorage. Then on to West Mills and Jack Murphy.

He knew the face of Jack Murphy as well as he knew his own—close-cropped sandy hair, near red in certain light, eyes pale green, nose short and straight, ears well-shaped, lying flat against his skull. A handsome man, Jack Murphy, in a rough-cut way. And big. Jack

Murphy was six-three, two hundred and thirty-odd pounds of bone and meat. And now Donavan wondered where in West Mills, another flooded city, he would find the man.

For Donavan there could be no fumbling search, no inquiring in the streets, no knocking on doors. West Mills had been his home town. Hundreds there knew his face and knew his record. One glimpse of his face and any one of them would sound the alarm. An escaped murderer was friendless, an escaped murderer had to move at night. And where, at night, in the flood-stricken town of West Mills, would he find Jack Murphy?

Donavan knew him well—habits, appetites and drives. In normal times, Jack Murphy spent three evenings in five at home. He entertained a lot in the big fieldstone and siding house he'd built on the hill overlooking West Mills. He was proud of his house, proud and jealous of it, as he was of everything he owned. He liked to stand in front of the huge fireplace, drink in his hand, a smile on his face, giving his impression of the man he thought Jack Murphy was. But he wouldn't be there, not with the big river on the rampage.

The dikes above West Mills were very old; they'd go as the Humboldt dike had gone. The streets of the lower town, the business district, the residential areas, north and south, would be under water, three feet and more. Along the edge of the main channel, at the anchorages and moorages, the full and brutal force of the flood would be felt the most. Jack Murphy would be here, certainly, at the Murphy Construction Moorage. All that he valued was here—floating pile drivers, floating cranes, dredges, barges, tugs and launches. He would be fighting the river to save them, fighting as savagely and as relentlessly as he'd fought to get them.

And how to kill him? A careful man would use a gun

and do the job from a distance, safely beyond Jack Murphy's reach. But what possible satisfaction could there be in killing the man at a distance? Where was the grip of the hands? How could the man know who was killing and why? No. He had to hunt Jack Murphy down and have him in some closed space, without a gun or a knife or club for either one. Donavan didn't know how it would come about, but he knew it would.

"Yes," he said. "And soon ..."

CHAPTER THREE

The flood smashed the docks at Greenfield and swept the pleasure boat moorages clean of everything afloat. The homeless and the hungry huddled around bonfires on the ridges above town—no one in Greenfield could yet even attempt to estimate their number. Existing telephone channels were jammed by those who wanted word of relatives or friends. Weary operators could only say, "Sorry, that number cannot be reached ..." Families had been split apart, children lost. A temporary information center had been set up, manned by volunteers. Not until hundreds of names had been taken did anyone realize there had to be an alphabetized file before any good could come of the work being done.

Greenfield's numbed confusion was reflected in other river towns. Bridgeton, already reeling, hastened evacuations. The Humboldt country was under water. The Humboldt dike had burst suddenly in a dozen places. Nothing definite was known of the fate of the convicts who'd worked on the dike with shovels and sandbags. The police were too busy with the problems of the living to worry about men who might reasonably be counted among the dead.

In West Mills, a committee of prominent citizens met in emergency session at 9:00 A.M. to discuss flood plans. Mayor Henry Balch presided, a stout, white-haired man whose hands trembled faintly. "West Mills has been included in the disaster area," he said. "I have been informed that help is on the way."

"So's Christmas," someone said.

"Gentlemen," the mayor said, "the flood crest will be higher than anyone dreamed it could be, the damage is already far worse than any early estimate. It takes time to implement relief operations on so vast a scale. The first efforts are naturally extended to the up-river cities where the immediate need is greatest." He wet his lips. "The governor assures me we have not been forgotten."

"What about medical supplies?" a doctor asked.

"Coming," the mayor said.

"We'll need tents, food, blankets, clothing."

"Soon," the mayor said. "Perhaps tomorrow."

He told them the evacuation of Mock Hollow had been completed. Seepage water was rising in the streets there. Present forecasts indicated that the lower town and most of the business district would be inundated to a depth of three or four feet. If the north dike held

"It won't," a deep voice said.

This was the voice of Jack Murphy. He had ignored the empty chairs at the long council table to stand before the windows. He was a huge man, solidly made, but he carried no spare flesh. He was roughly dressed: mud-caked rubber boots, a wool shirt, the sleeves rolled high on big, brown arms. His hands were dirty and there was a blond stubble on his jaw.

"Are you sure it won't hold?" the mayor asked.

"I'm sure," Murphy said. "I was out there a couple of hours ago. The inside slope is already seeping in fifteen or twenty places. Maybe more."

"How long do you give it?" someone asked.

Jack Murphy lifted and spread big hands. "Your guess," he said. "It can go any minute, or it can last another day."

"Bad news," the mayor said. His home was in the area protected by the north dike. Years of patient work had gone into the tending of his lawn; his begonias were famous throughout the state. "Bad news, indeed," he said.

"Thinking about your flowers?" Murphy asked.

"Yes," the mayor said. "For which I apologize." He pressed his hands hard together to stop their trembling. "Mr. Murphy," he said, "you have been most cooperative. I regret that I must make another request. We need your tugs."

"For what?"

"Rescue work," the mayor said. "The governor asks that we make an immediate search of all newly flooded land, in this area, and as far upstream as we are able. The dike failures were so sudden it is almost certain a good many people were marooned by rising water. They would be in grave danger."

"Sorry," Jack Murphy said.

"Anything less than a tug would hardly be adequate for the job," the mayor said. "A sound hull, a shallow draft and powerful engines are needed."

"No," Jack Murphy said.

"Can you refuse to save lives?" a cold voice asked.

"I can refuse to do the impossible," Jack Murphy said. His jaw was set and his blunt stare challenged the dislike that came to some of the faces at the council table. "Who knows where the channels are?" he asked. "Who knows what the depths are in those flooded areas? I don't. And my pilots don't. A man wouldn't be an hour in that flat country before he went hard aground. A sweet fix that would be, wouldn't it? —my tugs a mile from the river when the water went down."

"What of the people a mile from help with the water rising?" the same cold voice asked.

The owner of the voice was the town's leading banker, and Jack Murphy's blunt stare moved to single him out. "Are you opening the vaults of your bank to any flood victim who needs a few dollars? —not by a damned sight!" He swung his gaze to a department store owner. "Have you opened the doors of your store so that those who need clothes and gear can help themselves? —no, by God!" Jack Murphy's face was dark, his chest was big. "But what've I done? I've donated a fleet of trucks, two power shovels, three bulldozers, and I'm paying the drivers and operators overtime to man them! Isn't that enough? Isn't that my share?"

The banker, a small wisp of a man with white hair, turned to the others. "I will not say the equipment named by Mr. Murphy is not working as he says it is. But I would like to point out that it is working only in those areas necessary to the protection of his own river front property."

"Mine," Jack Murphy said, "and maybe ten million dollars' worth of other men's property on the waterfront below me. I say that what I'm doing is enough. You can't expect one man to carry the whole load. There are other tugs."

"They've been offered. They're in use."

"Then you've got enough!" Jack Murphy's face was black with fury. "I've got nearly a million dollars' worth of floating equipment on the waterfront. I stand to lose it without those tugs. And I'm not going to lose it! You're not going to get one of my tugs—not one! Make up your mind to that!"

The banker met his eyes squarely. "They can be commandeered."

The mayor's voice was desperate. "Gentlemen, please!"

Jack Murphy did not hear him. He pointed a blunt forefinger at the banker, sighting down it like a rifle. "Come after my tugs," he said. "Come after them any time you like. But I'm warning you—you'll need an army to get them."

And he left the meeting.

The midday hours passed slowly for the people in the flooded farmhouse in the Humboldt area above Lebannon. There was little for any of them to do. Even watching for possible rescue craft was useless—Donavan had made that very clear.

"I don't want help," he'd said to Elizabeth Matthews and Tom Sharkey. "Help of any kind would mean an attempt to imprison me again, and that would probably be fatal to me, as well as to others. I'll see that you're given every chance to stay alive; in return, you'll do the same for me." His voice had been matter-of-fact, his clear, dark eyes quietly sober. "If one of you fails me, that one will be dropped in the river before help arrives ... and that is a very solemn promise."

Neither Elizabeth nor Sharkey made any attempt to disobey, each knowing Donavan well enough now to know he would do exactly what he'd promised. Peebles, another convict, had no more desire than Donavan to be rescued. As it turned out, the order had not been truly needed. No rescue party came near enough to be signaled during the day—a small plane passed, high up, a helicopter was seen in the distance, two river boats passed, barely visible, on the main channel. The area of destruction was still spreading rapidly; rescue operations were still hopelessly outdistanced by the need.

The threatening bank of dark clouds held off, inexplicably, and for much of the day the June sun was out, full and clear. The people in the house were not uncomfortable; rather the springlike warmth the sun brought to the upper floor made drowsiness hard to fight. Elizabeth, whom Sharkey had finally persuaded to eat fully against the coming need, succumbed to the warm quiet and slept for several hours. Tom Sharkey, though nodding, remained awake in the sunshine that fell through the bedroom window.

In the second bedroom, Peebles said, "Gonna need that sack time," and got it at some length, snoring. Donavan, alone, seemed unaffected by fatigue or need of sleep.

He spent most of the day at the upstream window, silently watching the flood. The small outbuilding by which he'd measured the strength of the current was gone, struck by a floating log, collapsed and swept away. But there were other means of measuring the flow—the increased amount and the increased speed of the floating debris, the movement of the water at the house corners and the height of it, now almost level with the tops of the windows of the lower floor. Below him, trapped in a pocket between two bay windows, was a considerable collection of drift. Among other things, there was a saw log, two feet in diameter and twenty feet in length, and a section of shingled roof perhaps ten feet square. When Donavan saw a twelve-foot twelve-by-twelve timber come in, he turned from the window.

Using the hand-ax, he began the destruction of an inner wall. The noise brought the others. Elizabeth protested, Tom Sharkey watched silently, Peebles asked questions. "What the hell're you tryin' to do, chop the joint out from under us? What good is a two-by-four goin' to do you? What good is a handful of nails?" Donavan went on with his work without reply, methodically ripping out the wall, knocking loose lath and plaster from the studding. He split the nails out of some boards, saving the cleanest, strongest pieces of wood in a separate pile. Satisfied with the quantity at last, he put the nails in his pocket, the ax under his belt and went to the window.

"Pass the two-by-fours down to me," he said.

He climbed to the window sill, crouched there and jumped feet first into the flood. He surfaced almost at once, rising chest-high out of the water. A few strokes carried him to the pile of debris caught against the house. Separating the log and the twelve-by-twelve timber from the rest, he brought them along the side of the house to a point below the window on the upper floor. He looked up at the faces looking down.

"Let's have the lumber," he said.

Peebles handed him the two-by-fours as they were needed. With these, the nails and the hand-ax, Donavan fashioned the log and the twelve-by-twelve into the framework of a raft. The square of shingled roof was nailed down to serve as a deck, a length of barbed wire cut from a floating fence post became a painter. The finished product was crude and obviously less than was to be desired, but it was the best raft that could be built with the materials at hand. Donavan guided it around to the downstream side of the house, moored it below another upstairs window and entered the house again.

The others were waiting for him, silently now. In the mind of each, clearly, was the question of who was to go and who was to stay. Donavan did not answer at once. He spread a blanket on the floor and piled supplies in the center of it: some of the home-canned food, a cut of the beef, a kettle, a kitchen knife, a jar with a screw lid containing some of the kitchen matches. Then he gathered the four corners of the blanket together and tied them. Coming erect, he tossed the bundle to Tom Sharkey.

"You," he said. "You alone."

Peebles yelled, "Have you gone nuts?"

The others ignored him. Donavan's and Sharkey's eyes were locked, their faces were still. Elizabeth was watching the two of them, the color draining from her face. Sharkey's hands opened slowly and the bundle dropped to the floor.

"No, thanks," he said.

Donavan said, "You've got no choice."

"As long as I'm alive, I've got a choice," Sharkey said. "You may not think so, but you and Peebles are my prisoners. I don't leave my prisoners behind me. Nor do I leave this girl."

"Tom," Donavan said quietly, "this is the chance to live I promised you. You're going to take it, like it or not."

Elizabeth said, "I'll go with you, Mr. Sharkey. I want to go with you! And there's no use arguing with this man. You'll have to do what he tells you to do!"

The eyes of Donavan and Sharkey were still locked. Donavan's face was smooth, his eyes were quiet. Sharkey's lean face was taut and his eyes were chips of pale blue ice.

"Listen to me, Donavan," Sharkey said. "You're a man with sense, I know it. Use that sense now. You've done six years of a life term; you haven't got far to go before you're up for parole. You're loose now, but it wasn't your fault—I'll testify to that. And I'll tell them what you did for me, and for the girl here. That'll mean a lot to the parole board. It'll cut your time way down, if you go back voluntarily. The same goes for Peebles. There's room for four of us on that raft. And I know if you're along, you'll get us through somehow."

"I'm not going," Donavan said. "You're going alone."

"I'm not," Sharkey said. "We're all going, or we're all staying here until help comes. You'll have to kill me to change that. For the love of heaven, be reasonable, man! If I left you now, at your orders, you would be an escaped convict. I'd have to hunt you down. And I would hunt you down. With help ... with the help of every state and county and city officer in the country. And with the help of every decent citizen. We'd take you back, or kill you. You'd be one man against the world—you know that, Donavan!"

"I know it," Donavan said. "You're going, Tom."

"No, by God!"

Sharkey saw the beginning of Donavan's first step toward him and moved with a savage, planned suddenness. One of his hands caught Elizabeth's arm, a violent yank put her on the floor in a corner behind him. His other hand caught up a piece of two-by-four left after the wall had been destroyed. It was a splintered piece that could be used either as a club, or along, jagged and cruel-edged spear. Sharkey chose to use it first as a club, swinging it at Donavan's head.

Donavan was only able partially to block the blow. He took some of it on an upraised forearm, but there was enough force left as it struck the side of his head to open his scalp and drive him to his knees. A second, too hurried blow, missed his head and struck his shoulder. Still on his knees, Donavan waited for the third blow, and when it came he caught the club with his open hand. His fingers closed and held. Sharkey did not struggle to free his weapon. Against Donavan's strength he knew that would be futile. He released the club at once and bent to catch up another.

The movement brought his back toward Peebles. Peebles' knife was in his hand, and this was the moment he had been waiting for. He moved in, warily and slowly, and there was time for Donavan to throw the two-by-four he held. The spinning wheel of it struck Peebles' uplifted arm, knocked the knife from his hand and a splintered end of the board raked Peebles' face. He squalled like an injured cat and fell away.

Donavan was on his feet then. As Sharkey came up with another chunk of broken two-by-four, Donavan was on him smoothly and quickly. The wood was torn from Sharkey's grasp and thrown aside. A big hand caught the back of Sharkey's lean neck, the fingers closed and Sharkey was dragged forward. Another big hand, this one a fist, drove to meet the stumbling man. The blow caught the guard in the belly and sank deep. One blow with the power of Donavan's smooth bulk behind it was enough. Sharkey doubled, gagging breathlessly with the pain.

Donavan picked him up and carried him to the open window above the raft. He put Sharkey's feet through the window and held him there, sitting on the sill, until he felt Sharkey's breathing even out and felt strength coming back into the guard's lean arms. Then he shoved Sharkey's buttocks off the window sill and dropped him feet first to the raft. The fall was not more than six or eight feet; Sharkey was not hurt by it, though he still had not strength enough to stand. Sprawled there, braced on rigid arms, he stared up at Donavan.

"Let me take the girl," he said hoarsely.

"The girl stays with me," Donavan said. He turned back into the room, got the bundle of supplies and went back to the window to drop it on the raft. "Shove off, Tom."

Peebles was at the window beside Donavan, then. His small face was twisted, his voice was shrill with desperation. "Good God, Donavan! Think what you're doin'! You say you ain't goin' back, and then you turn him loose. Are you crazy? He knows where we are. He could meet a boatload of cops a mile down the river an' be back here before you know it! Why give 'im the raft? Why give 'im chow? If you got to let 'im go, drop him in the river an' let 'im swim for it!"

"He would be sure to drown," Donavan said.

"Good!" Peebles spat the word. "What the hell'd he ever do for you, you got to treat him so good? Let him drown!"

A sweep of Donavan's arm sent Peebles sprawling into a corner. His place at the window beside Donavan was taken at once by Elizabeth. She was so terrified she was fighting. She fought to get through the window, then fought Donavan who easily held her away from it.

"Let me go!" she gasped. "I want to go with him. I'd rather die than stay with you!"

Donavan brought her into the curve of his arm, pinning her arms against her body, holding her against himself. "No," Donavan said, "you'd rather live. And your chance of living is better if you stay with me."

Holding her, he looked down at Sharkey again. "Shove off, Tom. Now."

Sharkey knew the futility of arguing with the quietly implacable Donavan. More, his body was still numbed and breathless from a physical demonstration of that futility. He got slowly to his feet and loosed the barbed wire painter. The raft began to drift away. Tom Sharkey looked up at Elizabeth's white face.

"Don't worry, lass," he said. "I'll come after you."

"Wait!" Elizabeth cried. "Take me with you ..."

"And you, Donavan," Sharkey said. "As God is my witness, I'll come after you. I'll jail you or kill you, if I have to follow you till the end of time!"

Donavan turned away from the window.

He released Elizabeth, who stared at him with hate-filled, furious and tearful eyes, then turned and ran to the far bedroom. She threw herself on the bed there, sobbing. Donavan looked at Peebles. The small man had found his knife again. He was crouching on bent legs, knife in hand, staring at Donavan with fully as much hate and rage as the girl had shown, but when Donavan's quiet eyes came steadily to bear on him, Peebles swallowed his hate and his anger. He put the knife in his belt, shaking his head.

"You beat the hell outa me," he said. "Y'really do."

Donavan went past the little man without a word. He took his place at the upstream window again, watching each piece of drift coming down on the flood. His face was smooth. There was no sign of pain from the blow Sharkey had struck; the small, drying trickle of blood from the cut on his scalp went unnoticed. His attention was for other things.

The material of the drift was important to him, and he tried to identify each floating bit the moment it came into view. The dark cloud, coming on out of the distance, dragging a veil of rain, was important to him, and so was the hour of the day, late afternoon, with dusk soon to come. He was interested in the level of the flood, the way the water curled and sucked at the corners of the house, in the faint trembling of the floor beneath his bare feet. These were the elements of the calculated risk he had taken. He watched the development of each with a gambler's impersonal attention.

And fortune worked for him. In a little while, a boat came into his view, a rowboat, empty and riding with its gunwales nearly awash on the sluggish current. It was still a long way upstream. Left alone, it would pass the house nearly a hundred yards to the west. Donavan waited, carefully weighing his strength and ability against the distance and the strength of the current. When the balance was as equal as it would ever be, Donavan climbed to the window sill and left the house in a long, flat dive.

Peebles yelled, "What in the hell?"

He ran to the window. He saw at once what the task was. "Donavan!" he yelled. "Come back, you damn fool! You'll never make it!" He was not afraid for Donavan; he was afraid Donavan would be carried downstream, below the house, and he would be left behind. When Donavan ignored him, plowing on with his powerful overhand, Peebles turned from the window and yelled at Elizabeth. "Hey, you! Your boyfriend's gone clear nuts! Come here, take a look!"

The urgency of his voice, the near-panic in it, got Elizabeth up off the bed in the far room. Her face was tear-streaked and pale. She did not want to respond, and yet she was afraid not to. She went hesitantly to the other room. When she saw Donavan had gone and Peebles was alone at the window, she ran to his side. She was able to swim perhaps a little better than most women, and knew at once the size of Donavan's task, the odds against him.

"No ..." she whispered. "He can't!"

"Tell 'im to come back!" Peebles said.

Elizabeth shook her head.

"He can't make it," Peebles said. "Nobody could. Even if he gets that tub, he'll get shoved 'way downstream. Then how'll he get back here? I don't see any oars. Y'want to get left here?"

Elizabeth turned suddenly from the window. Her face was distorted; she pressed her hands to her temples. "Yes ... yes, I do!" It was almost a scream. "I want to be left here. Go with him! Both of you go and leave me alone!" She ran back to the other room and threw herself on the bed again.

Peebles said, "Is everybody gone nuts?"

He called to Donavan again, cursing him. Then he pleaded. Nothing he said was heeded. The big man went steadily away, making slow upstream progress against the current, his arms moving in an unbroken rhythm, the beat of his legs leaving a boiling wake. Now Peebles fell silent, watching. And it was a fight to watch: Donavan against the river and against time and no quarter asked. The onward drift of the boat was inexorable, the distance great. For the man to meet the boat in time to bring it in seemed clearly impossible. And it would have been impossible had there been a single break in the beat of Donavan's arms, or a moment's faltering in his determination. There was neither. Peebles watched with growing wonderment.

"Holy Joe!" he whispered. "Will you look at that guy!"

Donavan's path across the flood was slanting, planned to meet the downward drift of the boat. The meeting was not exact. Donavan's lifted hand missed the bow of the boat. He turned, trying again, and then it seemed he did not have strength enough to heave himself aboard. He went hand-over-hand along the flank of it to the stern. There he finally pulled himself up to lie across the stern thwart.

"I'll go to hell!" Peebles said. Then he turned to yell to Elizabeth. "He made it! That guy ain't human—he's a torpedo!" Almost jumping with excitement, he turned again to the window. Then the excitement gave way to despair. The boat was still drifting; Donavan was still lying across the thwart. "Pooped ..." Peebles said. "Too pooped to bring it in ..." He lifted his voice, shouting angrily. "Donavan! Get up! Get up, ya big ox! You'll drift past us!"

Donavan didn't move. The boat came even with the house, seventy-five yards to the west, and drifted past. Peebles became wildly frantic. He ran to the hall window and yelled at Donavan from that, then he ran into the bedroom and yelled at Elizabeth. She buried her face in a pillow. Peebles cursed. He caught up a chair, broke out the window on the downstream side of the room and leaned out, shouting, "Donavan! Bring it in! Bring it in!" In a moment, he realized the boat was late coming into view. Leaning far out, he saw why. The boat had come into the branches of a tree; Donavan was sitting up now, holding it there, resting.

Peebles swore at him. "He knew that tree was there!" he said. "Why the hell didn't he tell me?"

The boat was near enough now so that Donavan, with renewed strength, could not fail to bring it in. Peebles' excitement returned. "We got us a boat!" he said. "We got us a boat now—ya hear that, kid? We're all set!" He ran into the other room and began getting supplies together. The work didn't satisfy him. He raided a closet for clothes and found a khaki shirt much too big for him. His thin shoulders were lost in its vast folds, making him appear more ridiculous than ever. He got the knife from his belt, found the whetstone, and began to sharpen the blade with a feverish energy. Still, he was not satisfied. He needed someone to talk to. He went in and took Elizabeth by the shoulder and pulled her to a sitting position.

"C'mon, get up!" he said. "We're goin' to put the show on the road in a little while." He sat on the edge of the bed and began to whet the knife again. "You're goin' for a boat ride. You want to dry them tears and sharpen up."

"No!" Elizabeth said. "I'm not going!" She left the bed to put her back against the wall near the window.

Peebles grinned at her. "You ain't goin', huh—that's what you think!"

"I'm not!"

"Oh, yes, you are," Peebles said. "Donavan ain't goin' to leave a chick like you behind. Skinny or not, you'll do to take along."

"I won't go!"

"Don't you like the big guy?"

"No!"

"So how about me?"

Elizabeth's pale face was stiff, there was no hiding the revulsion in her wide gray eyes. "You are filthy, despicable!"

"So?" Peebles grinned. "How does that figure? All I ever done was a little thieving. This Donavan guy, he's a murderer."

Elizabeth stared at him.

Peebles' grin widened. "Ain't a thief better'n a murderer? Me, personally, I don't see anything wrong with bein' a thief. Some guys are born with a pot of money; some have to get it where they can. I see something I want, I help myself. Give every man his chance, is what I say."

"You're rotten," Elizabeth said.

"Have it your way." Ugly laughter moved in Peebles' throat. "But I didn't go up for murder. I didn't get mixed up with another joker's wife and break her neck. Donavan did."

Elizabeth stared, shocked and disbelieving.

"It's the truth," Peebles said. "He took her neck in his hands and popped it like a piece of celery." The sickness in Elizabeth's eyes was all Peebles needed to urge him on. "Le' me tell you," he said. "This Donavan was a wheel once—money, cars, a big house—what I hear, he had it all. Then the husband and a private cop and the uniform law bust in and find him with this doll dead in his hands. There's no way around it, he killed her."

"I'm not interested," Elizabeth said.

"So listen anyway," Peebles said. The twisted grin moved his lips. "He's big and pretty, an' he talks good; you think he's better'n me. So open them ears an' listen. I was in the joint when he come in. We celled together for a year, closer'n two bugs in a mattress. He plays it close to his belly; he won't open up, not a word. Me, I got good friends on the outside. I put it on the grapevine: 'What's with this Donavan? What's the score?' Pretty quick I got the whole story."

"Stop it!" Elizabeth said. "Stop it!"

"They got him for murder one—first degree," Peebles said, grinning. "I mean, he was really hooked. Open and shut. The husband was havin' her followed, see? That give the D. A. all he needed. He had the private cop's reports; he could show the jury what Donavan and this gal had been doin'. An' plenty of witnesses— the husband, the private cop, the prowl car bulls. He could show premeditation. They say it come out on the stand, the woman was tryin' to get loose from Donavan. He wouldn't let her go. He snapped her neck. The only thing that kept Donavan out of the gas chamber was some soft-head on the jury. They finally come in with second degree. That got Donavan life. He's a killer— that's for sure."

Elizabeth was silent, her lips pressed flat.

"Still don't believe me?" Peebles said. "My God, it was in all the papers, six, seven years ago. You must've seen it."

Elizabeth had seen it. She was remembering the newspaper pictures now: Donavan on his way to the courtroom, handcuffed to a police guard. Donavan, with the jury, at the scene of the crime. Donavan, arms folded, sitting on a bunk in the county jail. She remembered the pictures, but nothing of the trial.

There could be no doubt, however, that this was the same man.

"The doll he killed looked something like you," Peebles said. "Same size, same color hair. Her name was Murphy—Nan, Norma ... something like that. Plenty o' times in the joint, I hear him talkin' about her in his sleep."

There was a sound below the window. Elizabeth looked out and saw that the rowboat had come into the eddy on the downstream side of the house. It was an old craft, paintless and splintered from much hard usage, blunt of bow, square of stern, perhaps fifteen feet in length. A frayed piece of line trailed from the bow, a foot of water sloshed about inboard. The boat seemed to be traveling under its own power, but it was not. Donavan was in the water beneath the stern, sending it on with powerful shoves and swimming after it. Peebles came to the window.

"Some scow," he said.

Bitterly, Elizabeth said, "It's certainly better and safer than the raft you gave Mr. Sharkey!"

"Ain't that a tough break for the screw?" Peebles said.

Donavan made the boat fast to a porch post and came into the house again. He was breathing heavily. His short dark hair was plastered to his forehead again, water was running in small rivers from his big smooth body, dripping from his rough shorts. Peebles met him with a towel and a wide grin.

"That's what I call a job!" Peebles said. "Ain't one man in a hundred—a thousand—could've got out to that boat, to say nothin' of bringin' it in. Here ... let me dry your back."

Donavan took the towel and used it himself. "Bail the boat," he said shortly. "Get some supplies together."

"Sure ... sure." Peebles was all eagerness and haste. He ducked into the bedroom where the cooking had been done; he came hopping back with a kettle for bailing. "When're we goin' to shove off, Donavan? Soon's we can?"

"As near dark as we can make it."

"Man, we ought to get out of this joint. If Sharkey made shore and connected with the law, we're askin' for trouble every minute we stay here. They know where we are. They'll be comin' down on us like a ton of bricks."

Donavan stopped toweling his arms and shoulders and brought his level gaze to bear on Peebles. He said nothing, and there was no need to. The silent stare was enough. Peebles got out of his outsized khaki shirt, took the kettle and went down the stairs. He cursed loudly as the cold of the water bit through to his bones. Donavan finished drying himself and went into the half-wrecked bedroom. The closet doors here were homemade, fashioned of soft pine boards. Donavan used the ax to pry one of the doors from its hinges. He split away a board and began shaping a paddle. After a few moments, he looked up to find Elizabeth in the doorway, watching him silently. Her face was a clear mirror of her thinking; she was looking at him with a kind of horrid fascination.

"Peebles told you all about me," he said.

"Yes," Elizabeth said. "And I remember the papers."

"So now you know," Donavan said.

He went on with the work of shaping the paddle. And Elizabeth went on watching him silently. This man was a murderer—this was what a murderer looked like. He looked like almost any other man, Elizabeth decided, and then wondered if she'd expected the ability to kill, the urge to kill, to show as a black mark on his face. Of course not! That kind of thing would be a black stain in the mind, a mind behind an average face. Or perhaps in his hands. Now his hands took all her attention. They were big powerful hands; working with the ax and the wood, they were deft and skilled. She could well believe those hands could easily break a woman's neck—a grip, and twist and then a snap. Now her own throat began to ache and there was a sickness almost unbearable inside her.

Peebles returned, dripping. "Dry as a bone," he said. "Right now it is. But it's a rotten old tub; we're goin' to be bailin' half the time." No one gave him notice. He had picked up the blanket-wrapped bundle of supplies before he realized this, and then he paused, lifting his head to stare for a moment at each of them. "Say, what's with you two? Fightin' again?"

Neither answered him.

He set the bundle at his feet. "Donavan," he said. "I don't want to butt in where I ain't welcome. But I don't like to see anything go to waste, either. Don't get sore, now. But tell me this—do you want this chick, or don't you?"

"I don't want her," Donavan said.

"Y'mean that?" Peebles said. "Y'ain't kiddin'?"

"I mean it."

A wide grin came to Peebles' face. "Holy Joe! How about that? Here, all the time, I thought it was hands off!" His narrow shoulders went back, his thin chest came out. His eyes, alive and shining behind his glasses, swung to Elizabeth. "Baby, we been wastin' time! C'm'ere to me."

Elizabeth was shocked almost senseless. She stared at Donavan with disbelief, she stared at Peebles with horror. Her face was parchment white. She pressed back against the wall, fingers spread, eyes wild. Peebles came toward her, reaching for her waist. Fear exploded within her and she ran to the only refuge she knew, to a corner behind Donavan.

Peebles started after her, but Donavan brought him to a halt with a level stare. Peebles was uncertain; he shifted from one bare foot to the other, he worked his fists.

"Hey!" he protested. "You just said it was okay."

"I said I didn't want her," Donavan said. "I don't. She means no more to me than you do, and that is exactly nothing."

"Well, fine!" Peebles said. "So she means something to me. There's no law around. If they ever catch up with me again, they can put this on my tab. So what? I'll never know it."

"If you can come to an agreement with her, it's not my affair. But you'll not abuse her if she's unwilling, and she seems to be unwilling. Put the supplies in the boat."

"Holy Joe! What kind of talk is—" He broke it off, again stopped by the relentless stare of Donavan. He turned angrily to pick up the blanket-wrapped bundle. "Some people sure ain't got good sense," he said.

Elizabeth sank to the floor behind Donavan, shaken and sobbing. Peebles got the bundle of supplies in his arms and left the room. Donavan went on shaping the paddle, apparently oblivious to the heartbroken sounds the girl was making. In a little while the sobbing stopped. Her hands dropped and she stared at him out of brimming eyes.

"Do you always cry your way out of trouble?" he asked.

She didn't answer.

He looked at her. "A good girl, from a good family," he said. "Scared to death, and with reason. I suppose in my way, I've been as cruel to you as Peebles would be in his. It would seem that I've lost the habit of confiding, or making explanations. If it would help your peace of mind, I'll try to answer any questions you care to ask."

"You don't answer questions," Elizabeth said. "All you do is give orders!"

"Try me."

"Will you let me stay here? Please?"

"Definitely not."

"You see?"

"I see," Donavan said. "Try something else."

Desperately, Elizabeth said, "What are you going to do with me? You can't keep me in the middle of nowhere forever."

"This is not the middle of nowhere." Donavan continued to shape the paddle. "While it may seem like an ocean, with water everywhere, it's really only a river—flooding, but still a river. There's high dry ground on both sides of us. When I can be sure you'll be safe, I'll put you ashore."

"Where? When?"

"That I can't say," Donavan answered. "My needs, naturally, will come first. I'm going to travel as nearly in the center of the flood as I can, and only at night. I won't put you ashore until I'm absolutely certain that you'll be beyond reach of the flood and near help, and that I'll be safe doing it. I don't know when that will be possible—perhaps tonight, perhaps tomorrow night."

"Why didn't you let me go with Mr. Sharkey?"

"I built the raft with small nails ... all I had. I doubt that it will hold together in rough going. Alone, he'd probably survive by hanging onto one of the pieces. If you were along, he'd probably drown himself and you, trying to keep you alive. You won't drown with me. I can keep you alive without a raft and without a boat ... you should know that by now."

"How could you send him on a raft like that?"

"It was the best I could do for him while there was still time to do anything at all. Better, at least, than trying to swim with us—and I thought you and I would have to swim. The boat coming along was a lucky chance."

"You planned to leave Peebles?"

"Swimming, I could help only one."

"And now?"

"There's room in the boat. He'll go."

"But you know what he is!" Elizabeth protested. "You know what he intends to do with that knife!"

Donavan nodded. "But it's not my problem. What Peebles intends to do to society, what society intends to do to Peebles, is not my concern. Society revoked my membership six years ago. I can hardly be expected to worry about what may or may not happen to those who are no longer my fellows." He had finished the paddles.

"You're taking Peebles' side, helping him."

"And I'm helping you. It evens out."

"I'm not going, if Peebles is!"

"But you are," Donavan said.

He went to the window and leaned out. The boat had swung over against the house below the window. Peebles was bailing again. "Take these," Donavan said, and passed the paddles down. Then he went through the window in a dive that carried him over the boat; he surfaced and swam the few yards to the front porch. The roof of this was awash. He was able to climb from it to the roof of the house. From the peak, he had the widest view possible.

The veil of rain, the near darkness, had shut out every sign of high dry ground. There were lights a half mile or more upstream—the lights of a river craft of some sort, Donavan knew, probably a large tug. The lights did not change position in several minutes. The tug was aground or busy at some task. Donavan looked downstream. He could see beyond the barn and the grove of oaks to other scattered groves standing in reaches of open water. He mapped a course that would eventually lead to the main body of the big river and impressed it on his mind. Then he ran down the slope of the roof, cut the water in a shallow dive and swam back to enter the house again. Elizabeth was standing at what was left of the bureau. She had found a stub of pencil and an old envelope and was writing a note.

"It's raining again," Donavan said. "Hard. And it looks like it'll rain the night through."

"Just a moment, Mr. Donavan," she said.

There was a new note in her voice, an effort toward firmness. When she turned, Donavan saw that same effort in her face. She had reached a decision of some sort, but since she had only this moment reached it, there was not yet any real conviction in her voice, or any real confidence. The girl was not sure she had the strength and the courage to carry through the plan she had made. But the need was clear to her and she was going to try.

"You've decided what?" Donavan asked.

"To go with you," she said. "But not willingly... under protest. And I want something clearly understood. I'm going to do everything I can to see that you go back to prison where you belong. If I can signal anyone, I will. If I can talk to anyone, I'll tell them who and what you are. And when you put me ashore, I'm going straight to the police."

A smile touched Donavan's mouth.

"Is that funny?"

"Nothing like it," Donavan said. "I'm simply surprised. It's big talk for what has been a very small girl—if you're never able to do more, you've at least done this much. It's a credit to you. The note, I suppose, is the first shot in the war against me?"

"Read it, if you like," she said.

She handed it to him, and Donavan read: "To the owner of this house: if you will contact John B. Matthews, Rt. 3, Box 204, Biddleford, all damage to your house, other than flood damage, will be paid for. Elizabeth Matthews." He held the note for a long time, staring at it silently.

"Why don't you smile at that?" Elizabeth asked.

He did not answer at once. His eyes came up to meet hers. They were very sober. "It's not a thing to smile about," he said quietly. "It's a very decent thing for you to do." He put the note carefully on the bureau. "I'd forgotten there were people capable of such things."

CHAPTER FOUR

Donavan gathered blankets, folding them, and took them to the window. Peebles was waiting in the boat, small, impatient and angry, squinting up through the falling rain. He took the blankets and stowed them. "Come on!" he said. "Let's get this leaky scow on the river!"

Donavan turned away from the window. Elizabeth was waiting in the shadows of the near-dark room, watching him silently. He did not speak to her. Instead, wanting no mistake, he used a moment in careful thought. The tug upstream, the likelihood and the possibility of an approach; the movement of the floor beneath his feet, a definite sway now; and the time left before complete darkness—these were the things that occupied his mind. He weighed them carefully, balancing one against the other, finally reaching a decision.

Suddenly, Elizabeth said, "Let me stay."

"No," Donavan said. And this was his decision. "The chance of living would be too slim—for you and for me."

"I'll be all right here. I'm not—"

The sound of a whistle reached them.

"That—that's a boat!" Elizabeth said.

"A river tug," Donavan said.

Peebles yelled with sudden fear. "Donavan! Y'hear that? Let's get outa here!"

Donavan went to the window that looked upstream. Elizabeth followed him. They could barely make out the riding lights through the rain and gloom and intervening trees, but a searchlight beaming down on something close aboard was plain enough. Donavan could not tell whether or not the tug was closer than it had been—if it was, it was not by much, and it had stopped again.

Excitedly, Elizabeth said, "Now you can leave me … you've got to leave me! The tug will pick me up."

"Will it?" Donavan said. "I don't know that it isn't hard aground where it is. I don't know that it can, or will, come this way while there's still light enough for you to signal it, or that it can get close enough to take you aboard."

"Won't they have a small boat?"

"Probably," Donavan said. "And a small boat with an outboard motor could run me down in thirty minutes after they took you aboard." He shook his head. "I've got to be certain both of us will stay alive. I can't be, if I leave you. You're going with me."

"I won't! I won't go!"

Donavan took her arm. She fought him then, scratching, pounding his chest, crying hysterically. He caught her up, took her to the downstream window and handed her down to Peebles. She fought with Peebles, scratching at him. Donavan dropped into the boat and pulled her away. He turned to her and shook her roughly.

"That's enough!" His voice was harsh, his hands hurting. "I can tie you, and will, if I have to. Quiet down!"

She stared at him a moment, trying to find strength to fight him, then collapsed suddenly on the amidship's thwart. Donavan wrapped a folded blanket around her shoulders. Peebles, in the bow of the boat, was struggling with the line that tied them to the house. Donavan's quiet voice reached out to him.

"Let it alone."

"What?" Peebles was furious. "Are you crazy, man? We got to get outa here!"

"When it's dark," Donavan said. "And that will be risk enough. Keep your knife in your hand, cut the line when I tell you to. And then lay into that paddle."

Peebles cursed. But he took his knife from his belt

and waited. Donavan sat in the stern of the boat, his paddle lying across his knees. He watched the swiftly gathering darkness and he watched the house and he listened for any sound of the tug. These were elements of a calculated risk. They could work for him or against him, and Donavan saw no more than an even chance either way.

They heard two short blasts of the tug's whistle. Was it closer? Donavan could not say. Peebles began to swear in angry fear. Elizabeth began to plead. "Let me stay ... please. The tug will pick me up. I know it will!" Donavan ignored them both. He was looking up at the house. Long moments passed. He saw the roof line of the house move, then move again. One element of the calculated risk had worked against him.

"Cut the line," he said. "The house is going."

In his haste, Peebles fumbled the knife; out of fear of losing it overboard, he dropped it inboard beneath his feet. He bent in frantic search. Timbers cracked inside the house and the wall above the boat slanted suddenly, as if to topple over on them. Elizabeth cried out in fear. Donavan waited silently, looking past Elizabeth, over Peeble's bent back, watching the house. The sounds from within the house were constant now, shrieking, tearing sounds, not unlike cries of pain. The upstream wall gave way before the weight of water and flood-borne debris. Water spouted from the window above the boat, and the building began to cave in upon itself. At last Peebles found his knife and cut the mooring line. A deep-thrust, powerful stroke of Donavan's paddle turned the boat away.

Peebles yelled, "God, that was close!" Then he turned his face toward Elizabeth. "How about it, baby? Do you still want us to leave you?"

Donavan said, "Use your paddle on the port side!"

Elizabeth stared at Donavan, shocked, silent. She had not known the things Donavan had known. She had not watched the rise of the water, the gathering of debris, or measured the trembling of the house against the passing of time. To her, the foretelling of the collapse of the house was almost occult.

Donavan was thinking of the tug. The paddles he'd made were crude, narrow-bladed, the boat was sluggish and heavily laden. The best efforts of both men could add little to the speed given them by the current and could alter their course only a little. The nearest shelter was the grove of oaks, and before reaching it they would be long moments on open water. There was still light enough so that a man on watch in the pilothouse of the tug could find them with binoculars. Once seen, the beam of the searchlight would swiftly swing to find their boat.

They were still some distance from the grove of trees when the searchlight caught them. The tug's whistle shouted a series of quick short blasts. Elizabeth stood up, dropped the blanket and waved her arms. Peebles turned a frightened face to look over his shoulder. "Use that paddle!" Donavan said to him. To Elizabeth: "Sit down! —you'll swamp us, or fall overboard!" She refused. Donavan lunged erect to lock a big hand on the back of Elizabeth's neck and pull her down roughly across the thwarts. "Lie there!" he said. Hurt and stunned, she could only obey.

The searchlight clung to them, blindingly. The whistle sounded again. Donavan paddled furiously, driving the boat toward the oaks with all the power of his big shoulders. The last element of his calculated risk had worked against him. The tug had not been aground, it had been moving downstream and there was enough depth to float it here. If the pilot had courage, he could bring the tug to the edge of the grove of trees. And it seemed that he had courage. The tug was coming on steadily.

Those aboard the tug could not know who was in the rowboat or what their intentions were. The men in the pilothouse saw them as people who had fled the broken house at the moment of its collapse and were now trying to help themselves in a way that was not yet clear. Because of this, and the distance the tug had to travel, Donavan was given time to reach the trees. But once he had passed into the trees without any effort to make fast to one of them, and continued on, his purpose and character became immediately clear. He did not want help, and anyone who did not want help in this flood was criminal. A voice multiplied a hundred times by an electronic megaphone boomed out at him.

"You in the boat! —come out of there!"

The searchlight's beam penetrated into the grove, clinging to Donavan, but lighting the way for him, too. He found an aisle through the thick trunks and followed it downstream for fifty yards, turning there into another aisle that carried him deeper into the grove toward a clump of low-growing trees that would make a screen of sorts. He'd reached the screen, had gone beyond it, when the tug came up to the outer edge of the grove. He heard the clanging of engine room bells and the vibrating pulse of the engine going into reverse. The voice of the megaphone boomed into the trees.

"This is the law! Show yourself! Come out of there and come aboard, or you'll be fired upon!"

Donavan knew they could not be seen behind the screen of trees. Even the light here was blocked out to almost nothing. The big oaks had thinned, giving him some open water, and he turned the bow to cross it, driving the paddle deep. Peebles, in the bow, was digging at the water furiously; without turning, he gasped raggedly, "Godawmighty, Donavan! I can't keep this up. What're we goin' to do?" And Donavan answered, "The minute you stop I'll break your back!" The beam of the searchlight swung across the trees, probing for them, searching.

"This is your last warning!" the megaphone said.

To Elizabeth, Donavan said, "Lie on the bottom!"

She obeyed him, crouching low between the thwarts. A gun was fired—the muzzle blast named it a high-powered rifle—and Donavan heard the slap of a bullet passing over them, high and twenty yards to the left. A shot that wide was a blind shot; a shot that high was a warning. He drove the boat on, closing the last bit of open water and found trees again. The rifle began a steady fire, blind fire still, but now with no attempt to warn or intimidate. These bullets were meant to wound or kill. Some found their way through the trees at the shoulder level of a man riding in a row boat, others struck solid oak and were buried, still others ricocheted, whining angrily away.

Full dark was on them now. The beam of the searchlight, when it came near the boat, was more a help than a danger. The oaks stood thickly here. Light could penetrate them, but not vision, and the light helped Donavan find his way. Peebles had to put aside his paddle. He shoved the bow of the boat away from trees, he helped the boat along by pulling on low branches. Donavan drove on relentlessly. Branches came out of the darkness to cut at his face and chest and shoulders like whips, to scratch at him like claws. The rifle was emptied and loaded again and emptied again. A few of the bullets snapped by quite near, but most of them passed far away. No one was hit. In a little while, Peebles collapsed in the bow of the boat.

"No more trees," he gasped. "We gotta stop!"

Donavan did not stop until he'd driven the boat well out into the open water and turned the bow downstream. The map he'd impressed upon his mind while standing on the roof peak told him there was a stretch of open water here almost a mile long, moving with the full current of the flood. Now he put the paddle across his knees and turned his face up to the steady rain, mouth open, breathing heavily and deeply. The ripping voice of an outboard motor spoke out behind them, but Donavan was not troubled. They would search through the oaks first and before they were finished with that the current would have carried him safely beyond any reasonable chance of being found. Presently, he spoke to Elizabeth.

"Are you all right, girl?"

"Yes," she answered.

She got up from the bottom of the boat, wrapping the blanket around her shoulders, and sat huddled and silent. Fighting with Donavan in the house, she had been wildly angry, and then, in her helplessness, she had become hysterical; after that, with the wicked slap of bullets passing close by, she had been completely terrified. She was none of these things now. A clear, cold quiet had come to fill her mind. She found she could look at the dark shadow of Donavan without being afraid, and that she could think of Peebles in the bow behind her with only disgust. Something had happened to her in the last few minutes of lying on the bottom of the boat. What it was she could not say; she did know she was no longer afraid. She spoke to the black shadow that was Donavan.

"You're really very desperate, aren't you?"

"I want to stay alive, if that's what you mean."

"And die rather than let them take you?"

"Yes," he said.

"You're very lucky they didn't kill you just now."

"Or unlucky that they had the chance. Things could have worked for me. The tug needn't have shown up at all. The house could have stood until complete darkness and I could have got away without being seen."

"You knew the house was going?"

"It had to go. But I didn't know when. It depended on what wreckage piled up against it. A few big logs could have knocked it down in midafternoon. Again, it could have been standing at midnight. Ten minutes more would have helped."

"That's why you sent Mr. Sharkey on that flimsy raft—you were afraid the house would go with him still there, and you wouldn't be able to save him."

"It's better to take the slim chance," Donavan said, "than to risk having no chance at all. But let's be honest—I wanted to get shut of him, and had to get shut of him. Believe me, in anything I do, I'll keep a slim chance for myself."

Elizabeth said, "If you knew the house was going, why did you let me leave the note? To make me look stupid?"

Donavan was silent a long moment. Then he said, "What's the next best thing to the ability to do something? It's the clear and honest intention to do it, isn't it? And that's what your note was. I've seen so little clear and honest intention toward decency these past years, I couldn't bring myself to destroy your attempt. It still stands as a credit to you."

Now Elizabeth was silent a moment. "Are you playing games with me? Or am I hearing wrong? A statement like that from a man like you—what does it mean?"

An amused sound came from Donavan. "It might mean that even a murderer can be capable of a certain sensibility. I knew a murderer who was a thinking man ... he was executed." He paused, then leaned forward. "But tell me what's happened to you? I can't see your face, but you don't sound like that screaming hooligan we had with us a while ago."

"I don't know what's happened to me," she said. "I've been wondering. I don't seem to be afraid of you any more, or of Peebles. It may sound silly, but it's true."

"Maybe all you needed was a look at the worst to find out it wasn't as bad as you thought it would be. You nearly drowned, you met Peebles and me and you were shot at—altogether, about as bad as it can get. But you've survived."

"That may be it," she said. "I don't know. But I do know I'm through with screaming."

"Good girl," he said. "And how about fighting me?"

"I told you what I'd do about you," she said. "I didn't know then if I'd be able to or not, but now I know I can fight you. You're a murderer. You've got to go back to prison."

"Yeah?" Peebles said from the bow. "How about me?"

"You, too," Elizabeth said.

Peebles' laugh was shrill. "Will you get this gal?" he said. "All of a sudden she's full of fire and barbed wire. Gonna see us both back in the joint. How about that?" He leaned forward suddenly and caught her by the hair. A jerk pulled her backward off the amidship thwart. He held her by the hair and brought his face close to hers. "Let me tell you something, baby. You make one wrong move when I'm around, and—"

Both her hands went up, fingers hooked into claws. Her nails raked Peeble's face from forehead to chin, dragging his glasses off, digging at his eyes. Peebles squealed. His first thought was for his glasses; he let go of her hair to save them. Elizabeth twisted away from him. She put the amidship thwart between them and crouched there, her back touching Donavan's knees. Peebles found his glasses and cursed her.

"You'll pay for that!" he said. "Let me get you alone, and you'll pay for that!"

Quietly, Donavan said, "Hold your dirty tongue."

"Filthy worm!" Elizabeth said. "I'll spit on you!"

Donavan's hand dropped on her shoulder. "Steady, girl," he said. "Let's take it a bit slower. Like anybody else, you've got to grow up a little at a time." And to Peebles: "That's for you. Rough her again, and I'll collect for it."

"She clawed my face. She—"

"You heard me," Donavan said. "Lay into that paddle."

Tom Sharkey went where the river took him. At first, he had hoped to reach the west shore and help quickly, but the clumsy, deep-riding raft had borne him downriver and to the east. He had tried using a short piece of plank as a steering oar until he'd seen that the strains set up by his efforts would soon tear the raft apart. He had tried paddling, exhausting himself without measurably altering the raft's course. He had stopped fighting the river then. For the next long hour, he'd sat cross-legged in the center of the square of shingled wreckage that served as the raft's deck. Only his hands had betrayed his impatience; he could not keep them still.

The raft had moved downstream, now in smooth water, now in rough. It had passed groves of oaks and a flood-smashed barn—the timber frame of the building and a corner of the loft still stood, the rest had been washed away. Tom Sharkey had lifted his voice in a long hail. He'd got no answer; he'd expected none. Later, he'd seen a body clothed in prison denim, jammed in the submerged branches of a tree—Dortch or Rudisill or Avent, one of the men he'd lost on the Humboldt dike, another name to be scratched from the list of twelve. He had heard a brief snarl of motor sound and had seen the silvery flash of a banking airplane wing, low and far to the west. He had watched the sky, but the plane had not returned.

Lebannon was somewhere ahead, not less than three miles, certainly, nor more than six. Somehow, in God's good time, with God's help, he'd get to Lebannon, the county seat. The sheriff and the state police had offices in Lebannon. They'd lend a hand—men and boats and guns. They'd need guns to take Donavan. That one was a cold rough customer; he'd meant it when he'd said he wasn't going back. Peebles was nothing to worry about, not if you saw him first. He was pure hyena, dangerous only if the odds were on his side.

An hour ago, the sun had gone down behind heavy clouds. There was open water ahead now, a vast, wind-whipped sheet of it, pasture or crop land, taken by the flood. Tom Sharkey got carefully to his knees to probe for bottom with the plank. No luck. He searched the distances and found a single gleam of light.

"Somebody's alive in this mess," he told himself.

Tom Sharkey went where the river took him. Rain came with the darkness. The raft rode sluggishly, mauled by the heavy chop. Donavan had done what he could with the tools and materials he'd had, but the raft was a flimsy thing—sixteen-penny nails where spikes were needed. The churning currents, the battering of wind and wave weren't doing it any good. Tom Sharkey stayed carefully in the center of the shingled square. He watched the darkness deepen, keeping his eyes on the distant light that gleamed fitfully through the blowing rain. He saw the light blink out.

"Hey!" Tom Sharkey said.

And a shadow loomed suddenly out of the night—a tree, a grove of trees. No wonder the light was gone. Branches slashed Tom Sharkey's face. He fumbled for the plank paddle and lost it overboard. The raft slammed solidly into the trunk of a tree, hung there, wheeling slowly, wracked and twisted by the pressure of the current. It broke free, finally, deck awash, two of the two-by-four cross members gone.

The raft came apart. Tom Sharkey had time for one gulp of air before the water closed over his head. He went deep, rolled and tumbled by the current. He found bottom. He got his feet on the bottom, springing, and fought his way to the surface. The wreckage of the raft was all around him. The saw log was too big and too slippery to be of any use, the shingled square would not support his weight. He found an end of the twelve-by-twelve timber and clung to it with both hands. He turned his face to the sky, gasping for air, wondering what he would have done if Elizabeth Matthews had been with him on the raft. Nothing. He could not have helped her. He had all he could do to save himself.

Tom Sharkey went where the river took him, arms

hooked over the timber. Now and then he lunged upward, trying to find the light. But the numbing cold had him again and soon the effort cost too much. Time ceased to have meaning. He began to count aloud, needing the sound of his voice in the black world of wind and rain and water. Twice his thickening tongue faltered and he forgot and had to begin again. When his feet finally found bottom, it was a long time before he realized what it meant.

He clung to the timber, pushing with the last of his strength. There was grass underfoot. The water was chest deep, then it hit him at the belt. He let go of the timber, stumbling. He had come ashore. There was a knoll ahead of him. Beyond the knoll was the yellow gleaming of a fire. Tom Sharkey tried to shout, but the sound he made was small, a croaking noise.

"Easy," he told himself. "Easy ... now."

He moved unsteadily toward the fire, a lanky scarecrow of a man, half naked and blue with cold. He blundered into a fence and fell. He heard a giggling as he was trying to crawl under the wire. He wondered dimly who would be fool enough to giggle here ... and then knew the idiot sound came from his own mouth. His bare feet were on gravel then—a road, he'd found a road. The fire was in the middle of the road. Two men were sitting on boxes near the blaze. Tom Sharkey walked into the firelight.

"Hello ..." he said.

He had stumbled into a roadblock, one of the hundreds on the roads leading into the flooded country. The men were armed and suspicious, deputized farmers. One, Sam Jones, had a star pinned to his jacket; the other, John Tucker, wore a lettered armband. Jones wrapped Tom Sharkey in a dry blanket he took from a jeep parked in the shadows. Tucker poured black coffee from a thermos and laced it heavily with whiskey.

"We got orders," he said. "Nobody goes in without

they got it in writing from the sheriff. Nobody comes out without they tell us who they are, where they're from and how they got here. They don't want to talk, they try to run ... we shoot."

"To kill," Jones said.

"It's that bad?" Sharkey said.

"Mister," Tucker said. "I got a boy, high school age, I ain't heard from in two days. That give you the idea?"

"We both own farms in the Humboldt," Jones said quietly. "We had to leave most everything. What we hear, looters are cartin' off all that ain't nailed down." He had a shotgun in the crook of his arm. "When you're able, we'd appreciate to know who you are."

"A guard, from the state prison," Sharkey said.

He reached Lebannon at 10:00 P.M. He waded through knee-deep water to reach the courthouse steps. He walked down a noisy hall cluttered with refugees of all ages, tired and incurious—for him, the sound of a flood would always be the sound of crying children. He had to wait his turn to get to Sheriff Mike McFarland's desk.

"And one more," the sheriff said. He was a big man, red-faced, in a mud-stained uniform. His eyes were bloodshot, sooty with exhaustion. He looked at Sharkey's blanket-wrapped shoulders, torn trousers and bare feet. "At a guess," he said, "I'd say you're lucky to be alive."

"I had help," Tom Sharkey said. He dropped his sodden wallet on the desk. "My credentials," he said. "I had a crew of convicts on the Humboldt dike when it went out." He told the big man what had happened. "Donavan says he won't be taken alive. He means it, I'm afraid."

"That's why he kept the girl—for a hostage?"

"No. Peebles might, but not Donavan."

"Elizabeth Matthews?" McFarland said. "Yeah—I saw her name on one of the missing lists." He pushed the billfold across the desk, then rubbed his face with a weary hand. "We better fix you up with some clothes and chow and a place to sleep."

"I don't need sleep. I do need a gun."

"I can lend you a lever action .30-30 carbine, the only thing I've got left." The big sheriff looked at the bald and lanky Sharkey and shook his head. "You're hell for punishment," he said. "But in your place, losin' twelve prisoners at a clip, I'd maybe feel the same way."

"I'll need a tug," Sharkey said.

"Whoa, now!" the sheriff said. "I don't want a murderer runnin' loose any more'n you do, but first things come first. I got a town full of homeless people, flooded homes to guard, roadblocks to maintain. Half of Lebannon's under water—you saw it, you know what it's like."

"I saw it," Sharkey said.

"We got two tugs, both busy around the clock. One or the other will be goin' upstream. You can ride along." He rubbed his face again, an exhausted man, trying to stay awake. "Or you can go up with a light plane we got, a private job. We've been usin' it for recon work—no radio in it, but it's the best we got. I'll talk to the pilot. Come daylight, you can ride with him."

"The tug tonight," Sharkey said. "The plane tomorrow."

Bridgeton was in trouble. Two-thirds of the town was under water, the depth varying from six inches to ten feet. The business district was hard hit. Armed citizens and a few national guardsmen patrolled the streets in rowboats. A news cameraman got a shot of straw hats floating away through the smashed windows of a clothing store. City Hospital had been flooded out, the last of the patients evacuated as water crept into the halls. Temporary aid shelters were being established under canvas on the bald ridges back of town, in nearby grange halls, schools and warehouses, wherever a cot could be set up or a blanket laid down.

Oak Point, population 72, vanished completely in the night. The flood made a strange inroad here, creeping into the hollows above and below the town, encircling. The river was east of Oak Point; the first muddy fingers of the flood came from the west, at noon. At dawn, the pilot of a search plane found only a raging torrent where Oak Point had been. Fourteen frame buildings—homes, service stations, post office, tavern, general store and church—had been swept away.

Power failures had darkened most of West Mills, but the rain-lashed Murphy moorage was ablaze with lights. At 1:00 A.M., a man in the uniform of the state police, a captain, came gingerly down the cleated ramp from shore. There was bedlam here. Men were running on the walks. Some were fighting flood-borne drift, fending it away with pike poles and peaveys; others were dragging heavy cables; still others were carrying tools and supplies up the ramp to waiting trucks. The captain touched the arm of one.

"Murphy?" he said. "Where's Jack Murphy?"

"I wouldn't know," the man said. "Or care."

"How high is it now?"

"Forty feet even, the last I looked."

The state police captain moved upriver on one of the wide walks. The night was alive with a hundred sounds: rain and wind, the wide-open howling of gasoline engines, the deeper clatter of diesels, the yelling of a tug whistle, the suck and snarl of the river, the wind-torn shouts of men. The state police captain picked his way through a tangle of cable and new Manila line.

"Murphy?" he asked. "Where's Jack Murphy?"

"Where the noise is," a workman said.

Jack Murphy was standing in the center of a supply

shed, fury in his face. He wore caulked boots, tin pants and a sweat shirt stained with grease. He was doing something with a metal fitting, bolts and a wrench. He was listening to a battery-powered radio, cursing the radio.

"Who're you?" he said. "What d'you want?"

"Captain Hoppe, state police. We need trucks."

"So do I," Jack Murphy said.

The radio spoke of death and damage, estimating the number of people lost, counting the toll of major dikes destroyed. "Captain's Island, Blue Point, Littleboro, West Mills. Never in the river's history have so many been driven from their homes. Crest estimates now top the heights reached in the disastrous flood of '83 ..."

Captain Hoppe said, "We need—"

"No!" Jack Murphy said. "You lost three of my rigs when the dike went—that's enough!" He tossed the metal fitting to a man near the door, and that one vanished at a run. "I've got machine tools and gear to move out of here. I need everything that'll turn a wheel."

"Tools?" Hoppe said. "We've got to move the sick—"

Jack Murphy said, "That's your problem."

He turned his back on the captain, forgot the captain and went out in the rain-swept night, a flashlight in his hand. He checked the flood gauge spiked to a piling. Forty point two. Up a tenth and a half and still climbing. He was turning when a searchlight found him and a tug swung in beside the walk. A man thrust his head out of the pilothouse.

"Them anchors ain't holdin', Jack!"

"No excuses," Murphy yelled. "Just do it!"

"Take a look," the tugman said. "Tell me how."

The beam of the tug's searchlight flicked upriver. It was a pointing finger, not really needed; the floating pile driver a quarter of a mile upstream was ablaze with lights. Normally, a floating driver is held steadily in position by four anchor lines—port and starboard, fore and aft; it moves by taking in one line and paying out another. Not so the clumsy, top-heavy craft upstream. It was swinging back and forth, heeling in the savage current. A wild yell came down the wind.

"One anchor—lucky to have one," the tugman said.

"Damn you!" Murphy shouted. "Don't come cryin' to me—get it done!" He lifted a big fist. "If I have to come up there and show you how, you'll be a sorry crew!"

"Twelve hours—no chow. We gotta eat ..."

"Get up there!" Murphy yelled. "Move!"

Water boiled under the tug's stern. It pulled away, slugging into the current and the searchlight found the white glinting of piling between the distant driver and the shore. Murphy measured the work done against the total need, and swore again. He had a crew of babies, not men. That slanting, ragged row of piling was the beginning of a makeshift wing dam against which a sheer boom could be placed to deflect the drift and wreckage away from the moorage. Without it— A choking rage welled up in Murphy's throat.

"They'll build it," he said, "or drown ..."

He looked up and down the moorage, chest tight. He'd worked for this. While the nice guys, the soft guys, were home with their wives, Jack Murphy had got it all. One way or another, he'd got it all. Now the river and the gutless wonders on his payroll were trying to wipe him out—no, by God! Time was all he needed. Time to get the sheer boom in ...

He went up the walk, running toward the cluster of men at the upstream end of the moorage, the danger point. Beyond the men, beyond the pointed ends of the walks, were the anchor dolphins—clusters of piling, driven separately to bedrock, wire-roped together at the top for greater strength. There were five dolphins, from which the great weight of the moorage swung on heavy cables. The dolphins were still holding firm— no warning whip or sway; with luck, they'd bring him through. But the cables were awash, the web of them trapping and holding logs and timbers and planks, drift of a hundred kinds. Savagely, Jack Murphy cursed the weary men whose job it was to pry the wreckage free before the massing weight of it took the moorage out.

"Are you tryin' to ruin me?" he yelled.

"Hold it!" a rough voice said. Bud Collier, one of Murphy's superintendents, a stocky weathered man of fifty, had appeared out of the dark. "They're doin' the best they can. You can't get any more out of 'em, not even with a whip."

"Where're the rest of the men?"

"Gone," Collier said. "They're family men with wives and kids. They went home, them that still got homes."

"You let them go?"

"I did," Bud Collier said. He saw Murphy's heavy fist come up. "Do that," he said, "and you'll be short another marl. The way you do business, the way you talked to that state cop, you ain't got a lot of friends. Right now, you need 'em all."

"Friends!" The black and choking rage swelled in Jack Murphy's throat again. "The hell with that! — you're being well paid for what you do, all of you. You're not quittin', get that in your heads. Don't try to, walk off this job!"

"Who's to stop us?" Collier asked.

"Me," Murphy said. "You'll have to walk over me!"

The cold awakened Elizabeth again. She was lying on the amidship thwart, her head pillowed on her arm, her body twisted into an aching huddle beneath a rain-soaked blanket. She had slept for ten, perhaps fifteen minutes.

It had been like this throughout the night, a few minutes of tortured sleep, then hours of wakefulness. Awake, bailing the boat had been her task, and not an unwelcome one. The work was backbreaking and miserable, but each time she had been almost sorry when the task was finished for a time. The work had warmed her. Sitting idle, the cold gnawed its way back into her bones. Now her teeth ached with it and her body was shaking violently. The cold was the worst misery of all, she'd found. Far worse than being wet, far worse than being afraid.

The rain had not stopped throughout the night. It had been sometimes a downpour, sometimes a mist, but it had never given them a moment of relief. And there had been much reason to be afraid. The boat was large as rowboats go, but even a large boat was hardly more than a chip on this flood. Without light, they'd had to follow a blind course, suffering whatever the darkness and the river chose to give them. There had been a few reaches of safe, slow-moving quiet water, such as they seemed to be riding now. For the most part, they'd ridden the full and racing current, and it had carried them to the very edge of disaster countless times.

They had blundered into wooded areas to ram against tree trunks with a force that seemed certain to smash the boat, and then, caught in the roil set up by water straining through the trunks of the trees, they had spun and rolled and nearly swamped. Ravines, newly submerged, but not deeply, were separate rivers of rough water moving at near cataract force. Caught in one of these, the boat became a chip in every sense, pitching and tossing wildly, rolling the gunwales under.

A pile of debris had given them their worst moment. Saw logs and uprooted trees and timbers of shattered buildings had built a dam of sorts against the trunks of bigger trees, still standing. The boat had come into the debris suddenly in the darkness, turning broadside, and then had begun a rolling that could capsize them. Spilled into the water here, they were certain to be sucked under the debris and entangled somewhere far below the surface. Peebles had screamed his fear. Elizabeth had thrown her weight to the high side of the boat, wanting to scream, but not screaming. And Donavan, climbing out on the nearest half-sunken log, had heaved the boat across the log, out of the suction and had somehow fought it free.

That moment was behind them now, hours gone. And Lebannon was behind them. They'd passed the dark and stricken city, holding far out, knowing the place only by the scattered clusters of emergency lights set up at aid stations and the sweeping beams of searchlights that guarded the flooded business district. Now they were moving along a comparatively quiet stretch of water, miles below the city. And the darkness was beginning to break. Putting aside the blanket, Elizabeth found she could see the shadow of Donavan a little more clearly. She sat up stiffly, aching with the cold, shaking with it.

"Just a little longer," Donavan said. "We'll find an island at daybreak. Hog Island shouldn't be too far ahead, and it should still be above water."

Elizabeth was too miserable, too cold, to answer. She turned awkwardly and found the kettle she used for bailing. Between four and six inches of water sloshed across the bottom boards of the boat. She was glad of that, glad for the work. She drove her aching body to the task.

Peebles, in the bow, stopped paddling. "I'm tired ... man, I'm tired. My hands are raw meat. I got blisters on tops of blisters six inches thick."

"You can swim or paddle," Donavan said.

Peebles began to paddle again.

They reached an island just before full daylight. It was not Hog Island, or any other island Donavan knew; it was a piece of farm land that had not been an island since the flood of '83. Perhaps three feet above the flood, at the highest point, it was five hundred yards long and half as wide, one of many such scattered across what seemed a limitless expanse of water. There were a few trees, some undergrowth and an open area where grain was still standing. Donavan beached the boat and, with Peebles' help, ran it well up out of the water, partially beneath the overhang of the trees.

"Take the ax," he told Peebles. "Get some wood together. Dead wood, as dry as you can find. We don't want a smoke."

When Peebles had gone, Donavan turned to Elizabeth. She was still in the boat. The kettle had dropped from her exhausted hand. She was looking up at him, her face pinched, her lips blue with the cold. He lifted her out of the boat and put her on her feet. Then he took a blanket from the boat, wrung what water he could from it, and put it around his shoulders and her shoulders.

"I want you to walk," he said. "To get your circulation going. And hold close. I've been working all night, and there must be some warmth in me."

And there was. His only covering was the raggedly cut off pair of prison trousers, but Elizabeth found his chest and arms were warm. She couldn't deny herself this comfort, however small. She put her arms around him and her face against his naked chest. He did not flinch from the coldness of her touch. His arm went about her, bringing the blanket close about them both. And they walked in this fashion, clumsily, up and down, a dozen steps each way, until Peebles returned.

His arms were loaded with wood. He gave them his twisted grin. "Well, ain't that sweet!" he said. "While you two get cozy, I do the work. And I do it. I got dry wood—anyway it ain't green—and pitch to start the fire. Plenty've pitch."

"Start it under those trees," Donavan said. "And remember, watch the smoke."

"Don't worry about me," Peebles said. "I'm half Indian."

The matches they'd brought in a sealed fruit jar were

dry, and the pitch caught at once. Soon there was a substantial blaze. And Elizabeth, who had called cold man's greatest misery, now called fire his greatest blessing. She was warmed. and fed hot food. Then, while she was wrapped in a warmed blanket, Donavan spread her clothes on a crude rack and dried them.

Again, as it had yesterday, full daylight brought an end to the rain. The heavy overcast broke up and the morning sun came out to set things steaming with early summer heat. Donavan spread the nearly dry blankets where the sun could reach them best. There were four. Two he gave to Peebles. And he stood beside the other two and looked at Elizabeth.

"We've all got to sleep," he said.

For the first time she saw the blue shadows of weariness beneath the big man's dark and quiet eyes. His heavy shoulders sagged. The hand that rubbed the day-old beard that had darkened his face was not steady. He was not invincible then; he was as human as any other. She waited silently.

"You'll share these blankets with me," he said to her. "It's the least of the possible evils. And quite a small one, I promise you." A faint smile touched his mouth. "I'm known as a man who snores very quietly."

"All right," she said.

When the blankets had covered them, he turned his face from her at once and slept. And she slept. She awakened to find the sun well past noon. She did not move for a long time. She lay listening to the quiet breathing of the man beside her. He did not snore at all. She turned her head slowly to look at him. She could see him clearly now; he was disarmed by sleep. The beard bleared his features a little. The line of his short nose, the shape of his mouth, the set of his eyes were plain enough. Studying them, she tried to find some trace of cruelty and savagery and could find none. This was not the face of a murderer. This was the face of a man with a clean mind. And without willing it, she found herself trying to build a defense for him—the woman he'd killed must have been terribly bad, the provocation beyond endurance, or it had been an accident—then, recognizing the wrong in this way of thinking, she flushed with guilt. He had been fairly tried, found guilty and sent to prison. She had no right to defend him. Rather, her obligation was to see that he went back to prison.

She got up quietly from the blanket without wakening him. Peebles, wrapped in his blankets, was snoring. She went to the boat and tried its weight. It was far too heavy for her to float alone. Now the sound of a far-off plane motor reached her ears. The plane was so far away she was some moments finding it: a black speck, high and upriver, perhaps near Lebanon.

She left the boat and walked back through the trees to the edge of the grain field. The plane she'd seen, or another plane, might pass this way; there had to be some means of signaling it. There was no snow in which to tramp out a distress signal, no sand to mark, nothing white to hang, and no place to hang anything where Donavan and Peebles would not see it first. She walked into the grain and found her answer. The grain was broken down, a path was left behind her. Hurrying then, she tramped out the large letters "H—E—L—" There was not room for more, but the meaning of these could not be mistaken. At the edge of the field, she looked back satisfied. The grain that was still standing concealed the message; only a man in a plane could read it.

She returned to the boat. Donavan was awake now. He had built up the fire and had filled a kettle with water to heat for shaving. He had not looked for her, when he'd wakened to find her gone. She was a woman with a woman's right to privacy. But he looked at her now and saw what he wanted to know. She'd had no training in the concealment of guilt. Her wide gray eyes met his with an expression of innocence that would have looked false on an angel. He awakened Peebles.

"The girl's been up to something," he said. "I think she's rigged a signal of some kind. Shake down the island and find it!"

CHAPTER FIVE

Peebles rubbed sleep from his face, coughed and spat. He stared angrily at Elizabeth and then at Donavan. "Why don't you ask her what she did?" he said. "Or let me take her for a walk up the beach and ask her. She'll tell me."

"Do what I told you to do."

Peebles went away cursing. Donavan used the razor he'd brought from the farmer's house. He said nothing to Elizabeth. She stood helplessly beside the fire, watching him, waiting. Peebles would find the signal she'd tramped into the grain, or he wouldn't, and there was nothing she could do about it. After a half hour of torment, Peebles came back.

"Couldn't find anything," he said. "And I covered every foot of the island. Maybe you were wrong. Maybe she didn't—" He looked at Elizabeth. Again her face betrayed her. "Oh, yes she did!" Peebles said. "She's lookin' too damn smart!" He went to her, small and angry, his round eyes glittering behind his glasses. "When're you gonna learn that nobody gets smart with me?" he asked. "You're gonna tell me what you did, or I'm gonna mess up that pretty face. C'mon, now, what'll it be?" He waited a moment.

Elizabeth stared at him, hating him.

Peebles cursed her. His hand went out to take her arm. And Elizabeth spun away. There was no fear in her, only a sudden blind fury. The ax was lying near the fire. She caught it up and turned again, lifting it high. In her awkward hands, the ax was no real threat—a feint, a wild swing, and Peebles could take it from her—but the blaze in her eyes and the taut set of her face made him pause. Her voice raked him like claws.

"You slimy beast, you rotten, filthy creature ... don't put your dirty hands on me! Don't even try!"

Donavan said, "Hold that, both of you."

Peebles turned. "My God, are you gonna let this—"

To Elizabeth, Donavan said, "Put down the ax."

He had not raised his voice. There was no need. His eyes held hers, dark and steady, implacably commanding. She hadn't the will or the strength to defy him. She let the ax fall. Then, with a movement that seemed unhurried and without anger, Donavan took two strides and caught Peebles by the throat.

"This is the last time tell you to leave the girl alone," he said. "Don't ever try to lay a hand on her again. Do you understand me?"

Peebles could not reply. The hands about his throat had closed it. Donavan held him thus until the small man's eyes began to bulge and his face began to darken. Then he released him and let him fall away, choking and gasping.

"I told you to find what the girl did," Donavan said. "Keep at it, if it takes you the rest of the day."

Peebles stared up at Donavan. Hatred close to insanity was twisting his face; he could not conceal it. He got up and backed away from Donavan, then turned and went away. Elizabeth looked after him, shocked by the naked viciousness she'd seen on his face.

"He wanted to kill you," she whispered. "He hates you as much as a man can hate anything."

"He'd kill me," Donavan said, "or you, or anyone under the sun. All he needs is a chance to make a profit out of it, and a way to stay alive."

"You're not like that."

"Very few men are," Donavan said.

And Elizabeth stared at Donavan. The difference

between the two men was suddenly and emphatically clear. Peebles was a true criminal, degenerate, without any moral sense, worthless. No matter what Donavan had done, there was decency and kindness in the man. He'd shown that in a hundred ways. Now an impulse to help drove her to him. Her hands caught his arms to hold him facing her, her eyes held his, pleading.

"Listen to me," she said. "You can't go on like this. You're not mean and vicious and cruel. It's wrong for you to throw your life away. And that's what you're doing. Every decent man alive is against you, and they'll hunt you down and kill you—it's only a matter of time. Don't let it happen. Go back. Give yourself up. I'll speak for you, and Father will. He's an important man, really, and when I tell them what you did for me, it will mean a great deal."

"No," Donavan said. "I'm not going back."

"Is prison so bad?" she asked desperately. "You've served some time … six years, isn't it? And haven't I read somewhere that a life sentence doesn't mean life literally? With time off for good behavior, it's only fourteen or fifteen years. That means there's only eight or nine years left."

"I lost my good time when I set Tom Sharkey afloat," Donavan said. "But I wouldn't go back for even eight years. Eight years of living in a cage is too much to pay for the privilege of living a few years more. There's nothing here I want so badly."

"Don't talk like that! Other men—"

"Each man is different, girl," Donavan said. "Some will pay any price to stay alive an hour, and some don't mind prison at all. I'm neither of those. I won't go back."

"Look ahead of you!" she said. "What kind of life can you have? Running, hiding, never knowing who will turn you in, but knowing someone will—tomorrow, next week, the week after—knowing the police will come after you with guns. That's not a life worth having; it's suicide! Is that what you want?"

"I want to stay alive two more days. After that—"

"Why two more days?" she asked.

He looked at her steadily with his quiet dark eyes. "It's a personal matter," he said. "But very important to me. The truth is, nothing else is important to me."

"You might fail," she said. "I might be the cause of it."

"You'll try to be," he said. "I'm sure of that. And it's right that you try. You have that obligation. You'd be failing yourself and all the people like you, if you made any sort of compromise. I won't ask you to. But I think I can manage in spite of you."

"You won't ask me what I did this morning?"

"No," he said. "Because you might tell me. Then I would destroy it. Then you'd be guilty of aiding an escaped murderer to avoid capture. That's worse than a compromise; that's a felony. We don't want you to be a criminal, do we?"

The shine of helpless tears came to her eyes. "Are you trying to drive me out of my mind? Contradiction after contradiction—what kind of a man are you, anyway?"

"I'm Donavan, the murderer," he said. "That's all you need to know, all I want you to know."

Again Peebles returned without having found the message Elizabeth had left in the grain. He sat apart from the others, his face sullen and defiant and bitter with defeat. Donavan didn't send him out again. Clearly, this was something beyond Peebles' ability and intelligence; the island was small, he'd searched it a dozen times. Donavan took Elizabeth with him, then, and made a thorough search of his own. And he found nothing.

"You either made no signal," he told her, "or you're smarter than Peebles and I together." He smiled. "That last isn't flattering. I'll have to take the first."

And Elizabeth somehow felt like a traitor.

The plane Elizabeth had seen at noon remained

upriver, circling and sweeping back and forth. Sometimes it was out of sight and hearing for an hour or more, then it would return to circle perhaps a little nearer. But never much nearer. And, as the afternoon wore on, Elizabeth found herself caught in a strange conflict.

She did not want Donavan killed. But if the plane were to find the message she'd tramped out in the grain, men with rifles would surely follow, and Donavan would be killed. Killed solely because of the thing she'd done. She finally resolved the conflict in a woman's way. She would not destroy the message. If the plane found it, she would do everything in her power to attract its attention—Donavan had told her she must make no compromise. But there was no reason for her to wish that it would happen. No reason she couldn't hope desperately the plane would stay away until darkness came. With darkness, Donavan had told her, they would take to the boat again and continue downstream.

Two river boats passed in the afternoon, both far off, plowing a slow way upstream against the current. Each time Donavan watched Elizabeth closely until the river boat was out of sight. She was grateful that she could truly say she'd had no chance at all to signal them. When the sun was low, Donavan and Peebles made another meal, using the last of the supplies. Then the boat was brought from under the sheltering trees and loaded with the remaining gear. Elizabeth looked upriver. She could no longer see the plane or hear it.

"It seems to be gone for the day," Donavan said. "And that's a load off both our minds, isn't it?"

Elizabeth flushed and turned away.

Peebles said, "Yeah, and it's nuthin' but luck we didn't get caught. How long're you goin' to keep this dame around, with her doin' her damnedest to turn us in?"

Donavan answered the question, but only to inform

Elizabeth. He was looking at her, when he said, "If we have reasonable luck, staying with the full current, we should be near Johnsonville in an hour or so. Do you know the place, girl?"

"Not very well," she said.

"The west bank of the river for several miles on either side of the town is high ground. I'm sure we haven't seen the crest of the flood yet, but I know the town will be at least fifty feet above the worst of it. There'll be aid stations and plenty of people to help you. I'll have to put you ashore a mile below town and make you walk back. I'll need time to be on my way."

She shrugged. "I can walk."

Peebles said, "I ain't real nuts about riding that river again tonight. It'll be worse than last night. Like you say, we ain't seen the crest yet. She's come up a foot, maybe more, since we been here."

"You can stay," Donavan said.

"Not me!" Peebles said. "Another two feet of rise and there won't be any island to stay on. And I'm not goin' to roost in a tree. I seen too many of 'em floatin' down the river."

A plane found them then.

Whether it was the plane they'd watched through the day, or another, they could not know. This one gave them little warning. It came from downriver, flying upstream and flying low. Possibly it had been in a glide, motor idling, because the motor sound burst on them suddenly, and they turned to find it less than a quarter of a mile away.

There was no time to do anything about concealing the boat again. There was only time to reach the cover of the trees. And that was a close thing. Elizabeth, true to the promise she had made herself, tried her best to stay in the open. She twisted out of Donavan's reach, running, and when he caught her again, she threw herself on the ground, kicking at him. He had to pick her up bodily and carry her under the trees.

The plane passed directly overhead at an elevation of perhaps five hundred feet. The motor sound lifted, bellowing at full throttle, and the plane climbed steeply away. A wing dropped and the plane banked to come back for another pass. "They seen us!" Peebles said. "Sure as hell, they seen us, or whatever the girl did." And Donavan said, "The boat would bring them back in any case." And to Elizabeth: "Do you think they saw your signal?"

Defiantly, she said, "I'm sure of it! I walked in the grain and made letters. 'H—E—L—' It was all I had room for, but they'll know what it means. They can read it from the plane, but you couldn't read it from the ground."

"Sharp work," Donavan said. He was lying beside her, an arm around her, holding her pressed to the ground. The arm tightened and not in anger. "I underestimated you," he said. "You can be as tough in a fight as the next one. It's to your credit, girl."

The plane went over them, blipping its motor. It came back to pass over them once more, and then lined out at full throttle, going straight toward Lebannon.

Peebles cursed angrily. "Now what do we do?"

"That's not an easy question," Donavan said. He got to his feet and gave Elizabeth a hand up.

"Think he had a radio?" Peebles asked.

"Some light planes do, some don't," Donavan said. "I don't think that one did. I didn't see an antenna. More than that, I think if he'd had a radio, he'd have stayed to mark the position and called a river boat in."

"Okay," Peebles said. "So they had to go after help. But they'll get it, and they'll be back. We got to be long gone before they get here. I say let's go now."

"It needs thinking about," Donavan said.

He walked to the water's edge and stood there, looking silently upstream. The problem confronting him now was almost identical to the problem that had confronted him the evening before, at the farmhouse.

The elements were almost the same. How much time was left before total darkness? Would the plane send a boat? Could a boat be found and ordered out, and could it arrive here while there was still daylight? If he left the island now, what was the likelihood of encountering another boat in full daylight somewhere downstream? There was no safe course to follow, but which held the least risk? He made his decision and turned.

"We'll work the boat to the downstream end of the island," he said to Peebles, "and tie up again. Then we'll keep a sharp watch upstream. We can cut loose if we see a tug coming, with ten or fifteen minutes' lead."

"Why not shove off now?"

"And meet another boat downstream in daylight?" Donavan asked. "After last night, they'll all have a description of us. They'll shoot on sight."

Peebles rubbed his unshaven jaw. "You got somethin' there."

Elizabeth said, "You'll leave me this time, won't you?"

Donavan looked at her for a long moment. "If a boat comes from Lebannon before dark, looking for us—yes, I'll leave you. Otherwise, no. The boat may or may not come, this island may or may not be here tomorrow."

Many of the telephone lines in the Lebannon area were down. The others were held open for disaster work, calls of great importance and official use. To use them at all, a man had to furnish identification, to establish the importance of his call and wait a half-hour. The emergency shortwave net and the police radio were equally overburdened. To send even a short message on either required much persuasion and the very highest priority.

Tom Sharkey knew this well. He marked the position of the sun, when the light plane touched down on the Hillsdale airport, counting the moments of daylight left. There was not one to waste. He left the plane the moment it stopped. He pushed his tired body into an awkward run, through a hangar, past the airport office, down the road to the highway. The Hillsdale airport was a small, Sunday-flyer field; it was ten miles to the country courthouse in Lebannon.

A truck gave Sharkey a lift into town, an outboard-powered boat, manned by a state trooper, took him the last dozen blocks to the courthouse. The flood water had swallowed all but two of the courthouse steps. The halls that had been crowded yesterday were empty now. But Sheriff McFarland was in his office. A long table there was cluttered with field telephones. McFarland was using one of them when Sharkey appeared in the doorway. He put his hand over the mouthpiece.

"I got news for you," he said. "Wait a minute."

Tom Sharkey came into the room, slowly now, hatless and lanky, a bone-tired man, a scarecrow in borrowed clothes. The leather jacket he wore was too small; six inches of bony wrist and arm dangled from the sleeves. His shoes were too big, enormous army issue shoes. He carried the .30-30 carbine, the muzzle pointed carefully toward the ceiling.

"Sit down," the sheriff said.

He had aged ten years in twenty-four hours. His face was gray, the flesh of his jowls sagged. His uniform was stained and rumpled; he had slept in his clothes, but he had found time to shave. He pushed a chair toward Tom Sharkey and then spoke into the telephone.

"All right," he said. "Now listen to me ..."

Tom Sharkey unloaded the carbine, dropped the shells into his pocket. The sheriff was telling someone the courthouse meant the law to the people in his county. "They need me, they know where to look," he said. "I move out of here and set up shop in a tent, nobody'd be able to find me." He put his hand over the mouthpiece again. "Sandwiches in that box ..."

"Thanks," Sharkey said.

He had finished one sandwich, wolfing it, and was starting another before McFarland jammed the phone back in its case. The sheriff took a bottle of bourbon from a drawer and put it at Sharkey's elbow.

"I found them," Sharkey said. "They're on an island, five or six miles downstream."

"You're sure?"

"Yeah," Sharkey said. "I caught a glimpse of the girl—"

"Hold it a minute," the sheriff said. He used one of the field telephones. "Jackie," he said, "where's the *Bonnie-K*? Is she anywhere close?" A pause. Then: "Well, find out! And on the double! And call me back!" He put the phone aside and looked at Sharkey. "It ties in with the news I've got for you," he said. "Tell me what you've got first."

Sharkey told him. A day-long search—above Lebannon, off Lebannon and a mile or two below it—nothing. Late afternoon, back at the Hillsdale airport to refuel. An argument with the pilot, mean-tempered with exhaustion. One more flight, then, just one, and that one to hell and gone downriver, and then quit for the day. And the tramped-out letters in the grain. "The girl must have done it," Sharkey said. "Unknown to them. She tried to get loose to signal us, and Donavan—it couldn't have been anybody else—carried her under the trees. They've got a rowboat; that's how they got so far downstream."

"How was the girl dressed?"

"Overall pants, tennis shoes, gray sweat shirt."

The sheriff winced and shook his head. "Close!" he said. "Too damn close!" He looked at Sharkey. "The boys on the *Bonnie-K* thought it was three men. They ran into them, just coming on dark, up in the Humboldt country. They wouldn't stop, they wouldn't come aboard, so they were shot at—plenty!"

Sharkey felt sick. "Close is right. How'd they get away?"

"They got into a grove of trees," the sheriff said. "And it got dark at the same time. I don't care as much about your cons as I do that girl. We've got to get her loose. No telling what those cons will do to her, and the next lot of my men to run across them may not miss." He shook his head angrily. "That's a nice girl. Comes from a good family down Biddleford way. Her father's got a million friends. He's been in touch—"

The field telephone rang; the sheriff answered it. "Good! Fine! And get this, Jackie. Tell 'em they're going out again, right now. A man named Sharkey will be down to tell them what I want. They're to do what he says to do." He hung up.

"You're in luck," he told Sharkey. "The *Bonnie-K* is our best, and she just tied up at Higby's dock. Two of my boys are aboard to give you a hand. Whistle up that state trooper with the outboard, and he'll ferry you down."

Sharkey went aboard the *Bonnie-K* with something like fifty-five minutes of daylight remaining. The two deputies, tired and laconic, were in the galley, drinking coffee. The skipper and pilot was in the wheelhouse, waiting. He was a young man, still in his twenties. He wore his cap on the back of a head of curly dark hair. A look of cheerful defiance only partly hid the shadows of weariness that darkened his deeply tanned face. "You name it, pops," he said to Sharkey, "and I'll take you there … if there's so much as dew on the grass."

"Downstream, as fast as you can."

The young skipper yelled down to the engineer. "The man says all we've got, you dirty, old bald-headed Norwegian. Light a fire under that teakettle, y'hear me?" The powerful diesels throbbed and the tug heeled over under half-rudder and the sudden thrust of full ahead. The young skipper spun the wheel and grinned at Sharkey. "Any time you want action out of a Swede," he said, "just call him a Norwegian."

The big tug was fast, and it was riding the flood

downriver. Six or seven miles, Sharkey had said, and they covered that distance in very little time. The young skipper rang for slow ahead and turned to Sharkey.

"You've got your six, pops," he said. "Which island?"

There were a lot of islands, and if Sharkey had been a cursing man he would have cursed himself then. He had done nothing to mark the island with certainty. From the air, he would know the island at once, but from the wheelhouse of the tug they all looked very much alike. Most of them had trees, quite a few had small patches of standing grain. He had no idea which was the right one and told the young skipper so.

"Don't let it throw you, pops. We'll shake 'em all down."

"Try the biggest one on the left."

The skipper dropped a window of the pilothouse and yelled down at a deck hand. "Stand by the putt-putt. We're gonna hit the beach on that land to port!"

The tug went in until her bow found bottom. The deck hand manned the outboard-powered skiff and took Sharkey and one of the sheriff's deputies the rest of the way. It was not the right island. Sharkey climbed back aboard the tug. He looked at the lowering sun, his lean face stiff and gray.

"Plenty of time, pops," the skipper said. "We'll find 'em."

"We've got to!" Sharkey said. "Try another."

Donavan searched the sky and found only a lonely hawk, far to the north. The sun was well down, hidden by heavy clouds that were edged with yellow fire. The wind was cool and held no promise of immediate rain. Shadows were fast gathering in the distances. The plane had not returned. No boat had come from Lebannon.

"This is crazy!" Peebles said. "This is askin' for it!"

The rowboat was beached now on the downstream

end of the island, and Peebles was pacing near the bow with quick and jerky steps. His eyes were alive with impatience and anger, the tail of his over-big khaki shirt flapped as he turned. Downstream there were other bits of land like the one they were on, scattered widely across the flood. There was no sign of movement on or near any of them, and to him the way downstream looked safe. He came to stand before Donavan, craning his neck up like an angry rooster.

"I say let's cut out of here now!"

"When it's dark," Donavan said. "Or when we see a tug coming from Lebannon."

Peebles pointed a thin arm downstream. "Take a look! Do you see anything that way? Ain't it better to take a chance that way, than to wait here like a couple of sittin' ducks? It won't take 'em long to get a tug here from Lebannon. I say they're long overdue!"

Donavan didn't answer him. He turned to look upstream again. The tug was not overdue. In the confusion of the flood nothing could be called overdue; anything that was accomplished was remarkable. For any number of reasons, a tug might not be able to come after them at all.

Elizabeth was sitting on the gunwale of the beached boat. She'd thrust a stick into the ground at the water's edge some time ago. It was a flood gauge that now showed an inch of rise. She lifted her head to look at Peebles.

"Why don't you swim?" she asked. "You could use a bath …"

Peebles' voice went suddenly shrill. "Shut your mouth, you—" He was going to curse her, but Donavan's dark and quiet eyes came back to him, and the weight of Donavan's stare made Peebles change his mind. Instead, Peebles turned and walked a few steps away. He stood there, his back toward them for a moment, stiff and furious, and then he took the razor-edged knife from his belt and turned. Light glinted on his glasses.

"I had enough of bein' pushed around," he said. "I can take just so much, and that's all." He was talking to Donavan. "It's time you and me got a couple of things straight. Sure, you could take me, but I could cut you good before you did. Now ... you want to talk, or do you want to come at me?"

"Speak your piece," Donavan said.

Peebles jerked his head. "Tell her to take a walk."

"Stay where you are," Donavan said to Elizabeth.

"You don't want her to hear what I got to say," Peebles told him. "It'll foul you up."

"Nothing you can say will foul me up."

"Okay," Peebles said. "She's your baby. If you got to drop her in the river to close her mouth, that's your chore, not mine. Or I can do it, if you ain't got the guts. Now do you want to hear it?"

"Go ahead," Donavan said.

"All right," Peebles said. "You and me, we're in the same fix. We're a couple of real hot guys. The law wants us, and they'll shoot to get us. What's more, any Square-John with a gun will do the same thing on sight. It's gonna be a tough scrape to come through alive. What we need right now is money, clothes and a car. It wouldn't be any trick to get 'em. All these flooded towns ... a cinch. But no! You got to ride the river in that scow."

"You don't," Donavan said.

"If you do, I do," Peebles said. "I'm stickin' with you, Donavan. And now I'm gonna tell you why. I know where you're goin', an' I know what you're figurin' to do. An' I say don't be a damn fool. You an' me, teamed up, can cut ourselves a lot of cash out of the same deal. I mean a lot of cash. Enough to get you out of the country, and I got contacts to get you out. If you want to live it square, you can live it square the rest of your life on the dough we can get."

Elizabeth said, "How many children's throats would

he have to help you cut?"

Peebles snarled, "Shut up, you!" And to Donavan, "Hear me out, now. You're big and tough, sure. But you're a Square-John. You think like a Square-John. You couldn't shoot an angle in six months of trying. That's why you need me. I'll be on the level with you. This ain't a new thing with me. I been workin' on it ever since the day they put you in a cell with me. I see you're a big-wheel type. I think, 'What's with this guy?' Maybe you can do me some good. You wouldn't open up, so I put it on the grapevine: 'Find out about this Donavan.' I got a lot of friends on the outside. We stick together. There ain't a guy on the hustle we don't know about, and nobody makes a good score we don't hear about. The way it winds up, I know more about what happened to you in West Mills than you do."

Donavan looked at him steadily, silently.

"Don't believe me, eh?" Peebles said. "So listen. You and this Jack Murphy were partners. You got a big construction outfit—yours to begin with, and you took Murphy in. So you and this Murphy's wife are real friendly. It came out at the trial she was more like your wife. And that when she tries to give you the brush, you blew your top and killed her. You were headed for the gas chamber. Then some patsy fell for the cut of your face an' fought till the jury gave up on first degree. That got you an automatic life sentence.

"Who was it the D. A. had to make his case? It was Murphy and a private dick, J. S. Hallock. Murphy hired Hallock to tail you and the wife. Hallock got the goods—hotels, auto courts and your place. Murphy says he talked to his wife about it, and she sees she's a sinner and decides to fly right. She makes a meet with you to tell you to go jump. Murphy and Hallock get nervous—you're a rough character—and they get a uniform bull to help them break into the auto court where you and the babe are. Only it's too late. You already blew your top and busted her neck. Ain't that the way it went?"

Quietly, Donavan said, "That was the way it went."

"Now tell me something," Peebles said. "Who is this J. S. Hallock? He's got this credit agency. Need a guard to watch your payroll? —he'll fix you up. Investigation, skip-tracing, tailing—you name it, he'll do it. All on the up and up; he's a solid citizen. Sure, sure. But what else is he? You don't know, do you? But I know. And so does every other heavy in the country. Johnny Hallock's a contact man—one of the boys. Want to blow a safe in West Mills? Want to knock over a jewelry store? Show up with the right references, and Johnny'll finger the job for you—floor plans; burglar alarms, everything— and that's the guy that sends you up. I like to busted my ribs laughing when I heard. For a buck, he'd railroad his own mother."

Sharply, Elizabeth said, "What do you mean?"

"What did I say?" Peebles asked. "I said this, Murphy and this Hallock teamed up on your boyfriend here. He didn't kill nobody. But they hung it on him, real tight."

"You beast!" Elizabeth was standing, furious. "That isn't what you told me. You told me he did kill her!"

"For kicks," Peebles said. "Now shut up and—"

Elizabeth would not shut up. She went to Donavan, still furious, and stood before him, fists clenched. "What is the truth? I want to know. Tell me right now!"

"This is the truth," Donavan said.

"Why didn't you tell me?" she demanded.

"Quiet down, girl—"

"I won't be quiet!" Her voice climbed. "Answer me, do you hear? Answer me, or scratch your eyes out. Why didn't you tell me you didn't kill her?"

Donavan put his hands on her trembling shoulders. "Why tell you something I couldn't expect you to believe? The jury wouldn't believe me, and I did my best to convince them. Now I'm through denying it. It's a waste."

"But you called yourself a murderer!" she said. "'Donavan, the murderer'—I've heard you say it!"

"It's been my name—the way they spoke of me," Donavan said, "for the past six years. Maybe I'm used to it. Or maybe I like the sour taste of it in my mouth."

"But you're not a murderer!" Elizabeth's face was white, her eyes held angry tears. "I should have known it … I—I think I did know it. Now you've got to give yourself up! My father and I will help you. We can prove—"

Donavan shook her shoulders gently. "The thing is done, girl. The trial is over, the sentence passed, the appeals denied. Can't you understand that? Every door is closed. There's no way to open a single one of them again."

"There is! We can show that this Hallock is a crook. We could put Peebles on the stand!"

Peebles made a sound like ugly laughter. "Who's gonna put me on the stand? Who's gonna make me talk?"

"We can!" Elizabeth said. "We can subpoena you!"

"You don't say!" Peebles' mouth twisted. "Then I got to tell the truth, or I get my mouth washed out with soap—is that the idea? Don't be a dope, baby. If I popped off with this, I'd be stiff a day later. Johnny is a very useful character. The boys would frown on somebody who turns him in."

"I'll testify to what you've said!"

"And I'll say you're a liar," Peebles answered. "That wouldn't mean much—a con's word against a high-class dame. But Johnny's a high-class guy, and Murphy is real high-class. They'll call you a liar, and that'll mean plenty."

She turned. "Donavan, is he right?"

Donavan was looking upstream. The hawk was closer now, wheeling slowly on motionless wings, but there was no other movement in the sky or on the river. The reaches between the scattered bits of land were turning dark now. This time, Donavan thought, the calculated risk might work his way.

He said, "He's right, girl."

Peebles said, "So keep your face shut and let me get on with what I got to say. Donavan, how much is this Murphy worth? —a million bucks, two million bucks? And what's it worth to him to keep, say, half of it? The other half, ain't I right? We team up, you and me. We tell him, 'Split with us, and we'll go our way. Don't split and you'll go to the gas chamber.' He don't know I won't go on the stand and blow the whistle on Hallock. He can't take a chance. He'll spring our way."

Elizabeth said, "That's blackmail!"

Peebles' mouth twisted again. "What a dirty word! Why not say it's cuttin' Donavan in on dough that was took from him? A lot of what Murphy's got was Donavan's to start with."

"That's the way your rotten mind works," Elizabeth said. "You'd rather steal than do things the right way. And you don't care a bit if Donavan has to go on the rest of his life being a hunted murderer. You're filthy!"

"Rotten, am I?" Peebles said. "Filthy, eh? Well, let me tell you something, baby. You better talk the big boy into my deal. Maybe it ain't real pure, but it's lily-white next to what he's got in mind. Do you know why he's goin' to West Mills? No? Why don't you ask him? Go ahead."

Elizabeth turned her face to Donavan. Her eyes held the question; she didn't put it in words. Donavan's eyes met hers, dark and sober. He didn't answer the question.

Peebles laughed again. "Ask me, then. I'll tell you, I ain't bashful. I don't think the big guy was playing games with Murphy's wife—he ain't the type. But he was real fond of her. And he don't like it that Murphy broke her neck. Five will get you ten he's goin' to West Mills to break Murphy's neck. Want the bet? Go on, ask him. See if I ain't right."

Elizabeth stared at Peebles' ugly wicked face. The little man was completely confident, completely sure. He was grinning at her. Slowly, Elizabeth's eyes turned back to Donavan. His eyes were waiting for hers and the question that was in them. Again his eyes met hers steadily, and again the question went unanswered. But no answer was an answer! A denial would be so easy, and there was no denial. Elizabeth stared at the big man, a feeling of horror growing inside her.

"Oh, no ..." she whispered.

"Oh, yes," Peebles said.

"But that would be murder," Elizabeth said, and she was speaking to Donavan's silent face. "No matter what he did, you ... you, as a person, have no right to kill him."

"Murder one," Peebles said. "You're right as rain, baby. They'll take him for this one, and they'll gas him for it. Not that he gives a damn. He don't like the joint. He'd rather be six feet under than do time. But we don't want that to happen, do we, baby? I think he's a good guy. And you—let's face it, baby, you're nuts about him. One pass from him, and you'd sail. So what're we gonna do about it?"

Elizabeth was staring at Donavan. Yes ... yes, he was going to do it. How many things said so. This was the personal matter in West Mills. He'd said it was the only thing that mattered to him; after it he didn't care. This was the purpose behind everything he'd done: his staying in the middle of the flood, his implacable determination to reach West Mills. He was going to kill. And in this big and quiet man—she knew him well now—a resolve was as inflexible as stone. She backed a step away from him.

Peebles said, "Now, I say, if you got a choice between a little honest blackmail and a killing, take the blackmail every time. Killing's a nasty business. And it's poor pay. They'll gas him. But take my deal. He cuts himself a nice piece of change, and he's got a right to it. I put him next to the right people, and they'll get him out of the country. You can go with him. Why not? The two of you could live it up from here on in. And all you got to do is make him see the light. Lay into him, baby. For you, he might come around."

Jack Murphy read the moorage flood gauge and swore. The river was still rising; forty point nine now, up a tenth in the past hour. They needed daylight to swing the sheer boom into position, and the daylight was going fast. Murphy went up the moorage walk at a run. Bud Collier, dour and wiry, a weathered stub of a man, was pushing the sheer boom crew.

"How much longer?" Murphy asked.

Collier said, "You got eyes—look for yourself."

Saw logs, four and five feet in diameter, had been snubbed in alongside the walk—the raw stuff of which the boom was made. Bud Collier's men were drilling holes at each end of each log, chaining them together, end to end, fashioning a floating fence that would be towed upstream and eased into place against the slanting line of piling driven there. Three of the big logs still had to be drilled—not an easy task at any time, and now the pile bucks were stumbling, numbed with exhaustion.

"Ten minutes?" Murphy said. "Fifteen?"

"Make it a half-hour," Bud Collier said.

Jack Murphy turned his face to the sky and swore again. Close. It would be very close. Towing the sheer boom upriver would eat up time. It would be dark or almost dark by the time the boom was placed.

"You can hustle us up a tug," Bud Collier said.

Two of the Murphy tugs were in their berths, the *Jacksnipe* and the *Molly-O*. The third, the *Swiftsure*, was upriver, above the anchored driver and the newly driven piling, fending drift away from the moorage until the sheer boom could be placed to do that job. There was no one aboard the *Jacksnipe*; after thirty hours without rest, her crew had tied her up and gone home.

Murphy found a deck hand asleep in the pilothouse of the *Molly-O*—a blond and lanky youngster of eighteen or nineteen, asprawl on the deck, head pillowed on a folded arm. Murphy put a boot in the deck hand's ribs, not gently. Then he got a handful of the boy's jacket and hauled him to his feet.

"Wake up!" He slapped the boy across the mouth and saw fear come into his eyes. "That's better," he said. "Now—can you skipper this thing?"

"Some," the boy said. "I mean I—"

"What's your name?"

"Andy. Andy Anderson."

"Get her fired up," Murphy said. "I'll find you an engineer. You're going to tow the sheer boom upriver."

"Gee, Mister Murphy, I—"

"Don't argue," Murphy said.

Thirty-five minutes later, the completed sheer boom was moving upriver astern of the *Molly-O*. Slowly, at first, as the towline stiffened and the tug picked up the slack in the log chains, then faster as she settled to her work, diesel bellowing, white water boiling at her stern. Bud Collier watched her go, then turned his weathered face to Murphy. His narrowed eyes were blue and cold.

"Some crew you picked," he said.

Murphy said, "As good as I got left."

"A kid at the wheel," Collier said. "An engineer and a deck hand so beat out they're walkin' in their sleep. And what about Andy's mouth? You hit him, didn't you?"

"I woke him up," Murphy said.

"Yeah," Collier said. "And last night you slugged Gust Holm because he wasn't movin' fast enough to suit you. Thirty hours on his feet—one meal, no sleep—and you cave in his ribs." He spat on the plank at Murphy's feet. "We're gonna talk about this some more," he said. "After we get the pile driver home."

"Let's get at it," Murphy said.

But they were delayed. The floating crane's spring line was fraying badly; they had to rig another in its place. Then word came down the walk that a log was fouled in the cables at the head of the moorage, help was needed there. Altogether, it was thirty minutes before the *Jacksnipe*, headed upriver, Jack Murphy at the wheel. Bud Collier sat on the padded bench in the pilothouse, teeth clenched on a cold cigar.

The *Molly-O* was far ahead of them, well past the pile driver anchored at the offshore end of the row of newly driven piling. The *Molly-O* had the great weight of the tow to slow her down; the unencumbered *Jacksnipe* ran up on her fast. The two tugs were twins, tall and narrow of beam, twin screw jobs, diesel powered. The *Molly-O*'s running lights were on. She was just beginning her inshore swing, the sheer boom bending like a whip in her wake, when Murphy put the *Jacksnipe* alongside the pile driver.

Pete Rice, engineer, was abroad the driver. He had stayed aboard to keep steam up. He took the *Jacksnipe's* lines. Bud Collier got the heavy rope fenders into place. Together, they made the *Jacksnipe* fast against the flank of the floating rig. Collier went aboard the driver to help pick the anchors up. Murphy stayed at the wheel of the tug, listening to the clatter of the driver's winches, watching the *Molly-O*.

The *Molly-O* was in wild water now, fighting for every foot she gained. Her searchlight came on, pale in the dusk. The tail of the sheer boom was abeam of the pile driver, a lazy wooden snake, moving unhurriedly.

"Ho!" Bud Collier yelled. "Hit it!"

Murphy slapped the *Jacksnipe's* throttles open; her twin diesels went to work. He spun the wheel and the *Jacksnipe* leaned hard against the pile driver's awkward bulk, helping as the driver crawled up her bow anchor line, like a spider reeling in a strand of web. There was a moment of violent straining—steam winch and diesels pounding, the bow anchor line as rigid as a bar of steel—and then a lunging release as the last of the driver's anchors was torn from the river bottom and the scow-like craft moved slowly upstream. Bud Collier and Pete Rice dropped to the deck of the tug. Collier bounded up the ladder into the *Jacksnipe's* pilothouse.

"Hold her steady!" he said. "Don't turn!"

Jack Murphy said, "Why not?"

"Something's wrong." Collier rubbed mist from a window, looked upriver. "The way that searchlight's swinging—looks like the kid's in trouble."

"You're dreaming!" Jack Murphy said.

And in the pilothouse of the *Molly-O*, Andy Anderson wiped the sweat from his face with a shaking hand. What he should have done—he should've told Murphy to go jump. A big guy like that, big as a house, slugging a guy who was half asleep. Andy Anderson licked his swollen lips. What he should have done—he should've run like hell before he got squeezed into a mess like this. He could run a tug, sure. He'd done it, but not without the skipper around to head off his mistakes.

"Port," he said. "Swing the light to port."

Ben Root was with Andy in the pilothouse, at the searchlight control. Ben was a boom man, small as most boom men are, tough as a chunk of walnut burl— a grinning little ape, with a face stained beet-red by a hundred payday drunks. The very best you could say for Ben: he was company, but no help.

"Port it is," Ben said.

The searchlight didn't help a lot. Later, it would punch a hole in the dark, but now the white beam seemed to go out only a little way and vanish in the dusk. And the *Molly-O* was in wild water, the wildest Andy Anderson had ever seen. The big river had smashed the dikes upstream and chewed out a new channel here. Yesterday, this had been a low-lying spit of land; today it was a howling millrace. The river was throwing drift at them—clumps of brush, logs, timbers.

Andy said, "Them engines sound all right to you?"

"Purrin' like cats," Ben Root said.

"First time I ever had her out alone." Andy licked his swollen lips again. "I wouldn't fool you, I ain't real happy."

"Hell, kid ... you're doin' fine."

"What's that?" Andy yelled. "Ahead ... dead ahead!"

The searchlight beam lashed the roiled and churning water, swung too far, swung back. Andy clung to the wheel, leaning forward, peering down. The light finally found and held on the dark mass just ahead; a house, it seemed to be a house. Andy could see a sharp slant of roof; the light bounced on painted wood and window glass.

"Miss it!" Root yelled. "Miss it, kid!"

Andy Anderson spun the wheel, panic breaking in his mind. His only thought was to get the *Molly-O* out of the path of the bobbing mass of wreckage dead ahead. He spun the wheel to starboard, hard over, all the way, forgetting the *Molly-O* was tied to the sheer boom. The tug wheeled suddenly, diesels roaring. She pivoted against the tow cable fastened to her sampson post, well above her deck; for an instant she was a dancer at the end of a leash, trying to get away. Then she was broadside to her tow, battered by the wild current, heeling savagely, and now the great weight of the sheer boom took command. Andy Anderson felt her going. He was pawing blindly for the throttles, trying to close them, when the *Molly-O* capsized.

Bud Collier saw it happen. He was in the pilothouse of the *Jacksnipe*, field glasses at his eyes, when the *Molly-O* began her crazy turn. He saw the beam of her searchlight senselessly flail the sky. He yelled, "No, kid ... no!" and then the light was gone and the wildly churning tug was over, wallowing on her side. Bud

Collier held the glasses on her steadily in the instant of her death, and then the *Molly-O* had vanished and he raked the dark water, searching for a face, an upthrust arm.

Jack Murphy said, "That brainless fool!"

Bud Collier dropped the field glasses into their box and turned toward the door of the pilothouse. "Ease up on them throttles!" There was fury in his voice and in his eyes. "I'll cut the driver loose!"

"Do that," Jack Murphy said.

He let Bud Collier pass him, and then stepped away from the wheel to chop a savage blow at the neck of the smaller man. Bud Collier stumbled and went down. He crawled to his hands and knees, head wobbling. "Louse ..." he whispered. "Murdering louse ..." Jack Murphy hit him again. This time Bud Collier did not move or speak.

"Hey!" a voice called. "What's up?"

Murphy went to the door of the pilothouse. Pete Rice was on the deck below. "I was in the engine room," Rice said. "I heard somebody yell. What's wrong?"

"Nothing you can fix," Murphy said.

He went back to the wheel. He could see wreckage on the river's face—the sheer boom, probably. The *Molly-O* had come apart by now, mauled and battered on the river bottom—no salvage there. Far inshore, something white glimmered and was gone. Murphy wiped sweat from his face.

"I saved the driver," he said. "That much I did."

There were men on the moorage floats to take the driver's lines. Ben Root was there, a snarling man in sodden clothes. And before the driver was made fast, Bud Collier found Murphy on her deck. Collier had a peavey in his hands—five feet of seasoned ash, steel-shod, with pointed hook aswing.

"Root," he said. "What about the other two?"

"They didn't make it," Ben Root said.

"Clear out!" Bud Collier said. He was looking at

Murphy, speaking to the men. "We're leavin', every last man of us." There was blood on Collier's mouth. "Murphy," he said, and the name was a curse. "Try and stop us. I hope you do. I want to ram this peavey down your throat!"

CHAPTER SIX

The ending of the rain, if only for a few hours, brought relief to thousands of people in the flood-stricken areas. It was enough to be homeless, enough to be without shelter at all, or to be sleeping in tents, or to be lying on the floors of overcrowded halls, without the rain. The queues that moved slowly and endlessly toward the field kitchens, toward supply centers, toward first-aid stations were miserable enough without the rain. The rain meant deep mud and sodden clothing and shivering bodies and disease. To be free of it was to be helped a little, and to be helped at all was worth a thousand prayers.

But there was no relief from the inexorable brutality of the flood. Far north, near the headwaters of the Charles River, the Elk and the Black Fork, a drop in the water level had been noted. The mountains were free of their burden of snow. But the monster that was the melted snow had been loosed and sent on its way, and nothing could stop or contain it until it had found the sea in its own good time. The cities of Greenfield and Bridgeton were desolated and all but abandoned. The crest was here, surely. Downstream, the water was still rising, still spreading out to cover new thousands of acres, to destroy more homes and isolate more communities.

Property damage was beyond estimation. But the toll of dead and missing had fallen sharply. The paralysis caused by the suddenness and the enormity of the flood was largely broken. The people were fighting back. Organization, accumulated machines and outside help were their weapons. Threatened areas were cleared quickly and smoothly by evacuation teams. Disaster units had arrived in strength. Temporary shelter was provided in increasing quantity, emergency clothing was distributed at supply centers, field kitchens fed the hungry and field hospitals cared for the sick. Still there was much to be done, and still there were shortages. And people still died, because of the shortages, or because their shocked and numbed minds caused them to act in inexplicable ways. A man north of Lebannon burned his house to the ground rather than give it to the flood. A sixteen-year-old 4-H club member had to be chased and subdued by two men and loaded forcibly into an evacuation truck. His prize steer meant more to him than his life; the steer had to be left behind to drown. In Fieldview, a small community above Johnsonville, a young housewife hid herself and her child from the evacuation team that cleared the other homes. Her husband, a young doctor in the service, had said, "Take care of things, sweetheart," before he'd gone away, and to her stunned mind she would have been failing a sacred trust if she left their home. She did not leave. The flood entered the home in the early hours of the morning.

The boat carrying Elizabeth and Donavan and Peebles found its way haphazardly into the current that would take them to Fieldview at ten o'clock that night. Except that they could go downstream, bearing close to the west bank, their course could only be haphazard. The dark sky was filled with broken clouds, there was only a scrap of moon, and there were no lights or beacons to guide them. Even Donavan, who knew this stretch of river as he knew the streets of West Mills, found the flood had changed the shape of things almost beyond recognition. He guided the boat away from bits of land and other obstacles as they loomed up suddenly out of the dark, he drove his paddle hard when the way seemed clear, but beyond this he had to accept whatever luck and route the river chose to give them.

They had come away from the island where they'd spent the day without difficulty. Donavan's calculated risk had worked for him this time. To the young skipper of the *Bonnie-K*, Tom Sharkey had said, "I haven't been in planes much. What I thought was six or seven miles from Lebanon, was probably closer to ten or twelve." And he'd been right in this. They'd used the last of the daylight searching much too far upstream.

With the coming of darkness, Donavan had gone on his way again. Again, he had refused to trust Elizabeth's welfare to chance. The island might or might not be covered before she was found; he was completely certain he could put her safely ashore on high ground below Johnsonville—there was no choice. Elizabeth had come quietly, though not willingly. She was sitting now on the amidship thwart, a blanket wrapped around her shoulders against the damp chill. When the boat needed bailing, she bailed. In spite of Peebles' urging, she made no effort to argue Donavan away from his resolve, and had made none. Why try? The man was as immovable as a mountain. More than that, his quiet determination on murder—she could call it by no other name—had shocked her beyond any ability to argue.

From the bow, Peebles said, "Let's take it easy. We're comin' into something. Looks like a bunch of houses."

And presently they drifted in among the dark shapes of houses standing silently in water almost to their eaves. Donavan swung the boat in against one of them and Peebles made it fast. Donavan wanted to identify the community for the bearing it would give him. The houses were ranch-type for the most part, rambling, one-story buildings of recent construction. There seemed to be only residences here; Donavan, bending low, could not find the outline of any business structures of any kind. He searched his memory, his knowledge of the river, for the name of the place. It came to him, finally: Fieldview. Moderate to high-priced homes, a semi-exclusive district, with river frontage for boating and sailing—a little way above Johnsonville—it could only be Fieldview. Six years ago, when he'd gone to prison, this place had been little more than a scheme in a promoter's mind; now it was a reality. Six years was a long time.

Peebles said, "This's something we can use." His voice held a growing note of eagerness. "This's a regular little gold mine. You own a joint like any of these, you've got a few dimes. You spend it on silver, you buy a few rocks for the wife, a fur coat. And maybe when the river chases you out, you leave a little of that behind. How about it, Donavan?"

"No!" Donavan said.

"Wait a minute!" Peebles said. "Let's don't go clear nuts. We got to make a livin', y'know. Here's all this, we got some time, and there ain't a soul in miles—I say we ought to look around, at least."

Elizabeth said, "Thief!" It was a curse.

"Who's talking to you?" Peebles asked. "Donavan, we got to have clothes, don't we? I mean, how far are we gonna get without 'em. One look at us the way we are, they'll nail us. With decent clothes, we could be anybody. I say let's shake down a couple of these places for that much, at least!"

"Cast off," Donavan said.

"Man, be reasonable—"

"Cast off!"

Peebles loosed the bowline, raging and furious. Donavan backed water with the paddle, turning the bow away. Then they drifted. The water here moved slowly, but the streets were laid out in curves and to paddle would be to invite crashing into a house. In the bow, Peebles was ranting steadily, half to himself, about the stupidity of being honest.

"We got to have clothes! Is that too much!"

"Stop it!" Elizabeth said suddenly. "Listen!"

They were all silent for a moment, drifting. Then they all heard what Elizabeth had heard—the sound of a child crying. They were another moment placing the house from which the sound had come, and in that moment they had passed it. Elizabeth was on her feet.

"Turn!" she said to Donavan. "Turn back!"

Donavan was already using the paddle, the sudden swing of the boat threw Elizabeth to her knees. Complainingly, Peebles said, "Say, what the hell—" and Donavan's voice rapped at him, "Use that paddle. Bend into it!"

Driving the heavily laden, unwieldy boat upstream against the current was heavy work. They came into the backwater below the house, edged to the forward wall, then fought their way upstream to the front entrance. A jutting wall of the house set up another small eddy here. Donavan drove the bow into it, and Peebles made fast to an outside light fixture. The home was another ranch-type, one-level structure; the water level was near the top of the front door. And now the child's voice reached them clearly.

"Oh, Lord!" Elizabeth said. "What's happened here?"

Donavan was over the side of the boat. He sank into the utter darkness beneath the surface, swimming and fumbling blindly until he found the door latch. The door was not locked. It swung open sluggishly against the water, bumping against floating furniture. Moving in, Donavan found carpet beneath his feet and the water level at his chin. He could see nothing, but he could follow the child's voice.

"It's all right," he said. "It's all right now."

"Mommie ... where's Mommie?"

The child was lying wedged into the upper shelf of a floor-to-ceiling bookcase, a girl of perhaps four or five. She did not seem too frightened for herself—there was space enough for her on the bookshelf, and her mother had told her men would come—but she was hysterically determined not to leave without her mother. She struggled in Donavan's hands, as he held her high, wading back toward the boat, calling the woman. Donavan gave the child to Elizabeth. Elizabeth was agonized, not wanting to believe the worst.

"Where is her mother?" she asked. "She can't be—"

"I don't know," Donavan said. "But I'll find out. Peebles, come out of there and give me a hand. Lively now, there may still be time."

"Not much chance—"

"Any chance is enough!"

Peebles got out of his khaki shirt a moment before Donavan's reaching hand found him and came overside. The water was over Peeble's depth inside the house, but his awkwardly efficient swimming stroke was more than enough to carry him about. "Check the downstream walls," Donavan said. "This room first, then the other rooms. I'll find the kitchen." The kitchen, with its drainboards, stove and refrigerator seemed to him the most likely refuge. A woman could climb to the top of one of these and fasten herself somehow. But it had not happened. The woman had stayed near her child until the end of her strength and her will to live. It was Peebles who found her, finally, after ten minutes of search. He called Donavan from another room.

"Like I told you," he said. "Wasn't a chance she'd still be around. We'd have heard her."

"Let's be sure."

"I'm sure now. I've seen a few. This one's long gone."

And it was true. Donavan made completely certain of it—the woman was beyond any hope of resuscitation by at least an hour, perhaps a good deal more. Donavan held the lifeless body for a moment, then let it sink gently back beneath the surface. He waded to the doorway. The scrap of moon had chosen this moment to come out again; there was some light. He could see Elizabeth, a blanket wrapped around herself and the sobbing child; he could see some of the torment in her face.

"Nothing to be done," he said. "We're much too late."

"You can't leave her."

Donavan was running his hands over the area near the door, searching for the house number. "A few more hours here won't trouble her," he said. "To take her might trouble the child." He found the house number. "Remember this," he said. "The community here is Fieldview. The house number is 1738. We don't know the street, but this community is a small place. They'll be able to find it. They'll be able to identify the mother and the child. Report it as soon as you can."

"It's terrible ..." Elizabeth whispered.

"And only one of hundreds, I'm afraid," Donavan said. He turned. "Peebles! We're shoving off!"

From the dark interior of the house, Peebles said, "Be right with you." And he came a moment later, swimming hurriedly and clumsily. He caught the gunwale of the boat and heaved himself into the bow of the boat. He shook water from himself, he swore about the cold and he made a fuss getting into his khaki shirt again.

"Let's go!" he said. "Let's get the show on the road!"

Donavan had begun to move toward the stern. Now he turned back. He stared at the dark shape of Peebles for a moment. Then he swam to the bow, his hands went up and caught the bow and he heaved himself up across it, then turned to drop his feet inboard. Now he was facing Peebles.

"What did you do in there?" he asked.

"Do?" Peebles was startled. "Whatta yuh mean? I—"

"What did you take?"

"Me? I didn't take nuthin'! There wasn't nuthin'—"

"There was a ring."

"Hey! You don't think I'd—"

"I can go look."

Elizabeth's voice was almost a shriek. "Oh, no!"

The sound frightened Peebles, he twisted, yelling at her. "Shut up! What're you tryin' to do?—drive me nuts? It ain't none of your business." He faced Donavan again. "Get some sense, will yuh? What good to leave it there? For somebody else? It's a big rock, maybe a thousand bucks' worth. And she sure as hell ain't got any more use for it."

Donavan held out his hand. "Give it to me."

Peebles began a protest, then changed his mind. "Sure," he said, "Sure, you keep it and we'll split later." He put a diamond engagement ring in Donavan's hand. "See for yourself. It'll go a thousand bucks, maybe more."

Donavan put the ring in a pocket. Then he stood up and his big hands went out suddenly and caught Peebles' arms just above the elbows. Peebles squealed in sudden fear. He struggled to reach the knife in his belt and failed. The boat rocked dangerously. Donavan lifted Peebles into the air and heaved him away. Peebles hit the water on his back, legs thrashing, and sank. The current carried him beyond the stern of the boat before he surfaced again. He splashed clumsily, he called out, pleading. Donavan stood silent and motionless until Peebles was carried out of sight into the darkness.

Choked, Elizabeth asked, "Will he drown?"

"Not likely," Donavan said.

Then he dropped into the water and went back inside the house. When he returned, he loosed the painter, swung the boat and climbed into the stern. He did not take up the paddle at once. He let the boat drift, and sat with his head bent and his arms resting on his knees.

Elizabeth said, "You put the ring back?"

"I put it back." He didn't tell her he'd had to put it on the right hand. "That Peebles," he said. "I pulled him out of the river, and I put him back in the river." He shook his head. "But that doesn't clean me, does it?"

"No," Elizabeth said. "No, it doesn't."

"Is the child all right?"

"Yes ..." The child was lying quietly against Elizabeth's breast under the blanket, clinging to her tightly. Perhaps Elizabeth's female form was somehow taking the place of her lost mother in these shocked moments. "She's exhausted. I don't think she'll be able to stay awake. But helping her doesn't clean you either."

"Of course not," Donavan said.

A house appeared out of the shadow. Donavan took up the paddle to turn the bow of the boat away. The current had swept Peebles against this same house. He heard them and called out, but Donavan drove on downstream until the voice of Peebles was lost behind him. Then he rested, using the paddle only to guide them away from obstacles, letting the current carry them.

Elizabeth could not see his face, only the pale outline of it. Yet it seemed to her, suddenly, that she could see him now more clearly than ever before. She was sure she knew what was in his mind. The affair just past had affected him deeply. It had shaken him emotionally, it had shaken the confidence he'd had in himself, in his position and in his purpose. Perhaps he knew why he was shaken, perhaps not. But Elizabeth was certain she knew why.

Robbing the dead is the lowest form of human degradation. Peebles had done it, not Donavan. But Donavan had allowed himself to be associated with Peebles, and in helping Peebles had made the act possible. So was he not one with Peebles? No! But if he was not one with Peebles, what was he? Neutral, he had said. The conflict between society and the like of Peebles did not concern him. Then why was he affected? Why did he feel unclean? Again, Elizabeth was sure she could supply the answer.

Donavan's perspective had been distorted; his sense of values was out of balance. And understandably. A man of normal virtue, a clean man, he had been falsely accused of murder, disgraced and sent to prison for life—enough to warp the thinking of any man to some degree. Not being an evil man, Donavan would turn his back on evil. Having been horribly injured by the good he had turned his back on the good. What had been left for him? A middle way, a neutral way. In other years, he would have seen the idea was clearly false. There is no middle way; no man can walk completely alone. But after the disgrace, the injustice, the six years in prison, he hadn't been able to see it. Perhaps now, after the affair in the house, he was beginning to see it.

"You're a fool," she said.

"So?"

"You're sitting there feeling rotten," she said. "You're arguing with yourself. You're trying to persuade yourself that none of it was your fault. Or your responsibility. You're saying that Peebles meant no more to you than a ... a dog, or a cat. That you helped him, just as you would have helped a dog or a cat, and for the same reason. Isn't that right?"

After a moment, Donavan said, "It's very close."

Elizabeth felt the warmth of triumph. She had been right. The inscrutable Donavan was not inscrutable at all. She had looked into his mind. She knew who he was and what he was. He was a strong man, both in mind and body, with enormous capabilities ... and he needed help. Her help. Now every shred of fear and resentment fell away, and she became conscious of a deep need within herself: she wanted desperately to help him, she had to help him at whatever cost. The child was asleep in her arms. She spoke softly so as not to awaken her, but she spoke with cold and deliberate scorn.

"And I say you're a fool! You know perfectly well what

you should have done about Peebles. It's no use trying to deny it. You know!"

"And what should I have done?"

"He's a criminal, as depraved as a man can get," she said. "He belongs in prison, and well you know it. It was your job, the job of any decent man, to see that he went back to prison. You could have put him there, and should have put him there, even if it meant going back yourself. You had no right to help him. And you had no right to let him go now—no more than you would have the right to turn a mad dog loose upon society."

"Society's problems are not mine!"

"So you said before!" Elizabeth's voice flayed him. "And I've never heard a more ridiculous or idiotic statement in my life! It's an absolute lie!"

"I assure you it isn't."

"I'll show you it is!" Elizabeth said. "You've shown me a dozen times. You're through with society—what rot! Why did you help me? You could have gone on and nobody would even know you were alive. Why did you help Mr. Sharkey? He'll never rest now until he takes you back or kills you. You could have left him to die. Why didn't you harm me? And if you didn't want me, why didn't you let Peebles have me? Why did you help this child? Why did you give a ring back to a dead woman? We're members of society and these were our problems. Did you turn your back on us? —no! You helped us. Are you going to tell me you don't know why?"

Donavan was silent.

"You're one of us!" Elizabeth said. "That's why. You can't change your spots any more than a leopard can. You were never mean, vicious or cruel. You never can be. You're a decent man to the very marrow of your bones. Deny it, if you can!"

"I'm a murderer," Donavan said. "Is that decent?"

"You killed no one."

"I'm going to," Donavan said. "It's the same thing."

"Until it happens, it's not!" Elizabeth said fiercely. "And I'm not going to let it happen. I'm going to stop you somehow. If I can't stop you with reason, I'll stop you with the police. But listen to reason, first. You think what you're going to do is right. You've all sorts of proof that it is, I'm sure—proof that seems valid to you. But I know it's false. When I make you see that, you won't want to kill anyone."

"You can try," Donavan said.

"I will. You won't like what I have to say, but listen just the same. You're not in your right mind—that's the plain and simple truth. I don't mean you're insane. I mean when they did the horrible thing they did to you, you got turned around. You're seeing things backwards, or upside down, or something. And it all seems real and sensible and clear to you—you're used to seeing it that way now, you believe it's true. But it's a lie. Any normal person would tell you so. I'm normal. No one has hurt me. I can see clearly, and I know exactly what you should do."

"And that is?"

"You've got to give yourself up," Elizabeth said. "Go back to prison. Say to yourself you will serve whatever time you must—the full sentence, if you have to. Then, when you get out, devote the rest of your life to righting the wrong. You can do it! I know you can. When you've done it, there won't be any blood on your hands. And you'll be alive. This is the right way, Donavan. The only decent way. Can't you see it?"

"No, I can't," Donavan said. "The walls of the prison block my view. I told you before I won't live behind bars. I'm through with being caged."

"But it's different now," Elizabeth said. "You're not alone now. I don't know what I mean to you—nothing but trouble, I guess. But I— How do I say it? I—I don't know. But I know this: I'll die a little when you go back to prison, and I'll die a little more each day they keep you there. I won't, I couldn't, rest a minute while you're there. I told you my father is an important man, and he is. When I tell him what you did for me, and what you mean to me, he'll move heaven and earth to set you free, And he will set you free, I promise he will!"

"He couldn't possibly."

"Donavan, in the name of heaven!" Elizabeth said. "We know you didn't murder that woman. We know who did. You can't tell me it's impossible to prove the truth. There must be a way, there's got to be a way. No one can commit a crime like that and get away scot-free."

"They can and did," Donavan said. "I wasn't important and I wasn't wealthy. But I had more than enough money and more than enough friends who believed in me as strongly as you believe in me. And I had good lawyers. We all did everything in our power and failed. Your father would fail as we did."

"You don't know him!"

"I know the impossible when I see it."

The current had carried them into fast-moving, open water again. A cool wind, heavy with the muddy odor of the flood, began to blow in their faces. Donovan bent to find the kettle and bailed the boat free of water again. Then he took up the paddle. There was a difference in the way he worked the blade now, a new purpose, and, fearfully, Elizabeth turned to look downstream. The reason was clear at once. A glow was lighting the sky to the south and west. Elizabeth turned back.

"Johnsonville?" she asked.

"That's right."

And Elizabeth felt the sudden ache of desperation. "Don't paddle," she said. "We'll be there soon enough. Give me that much, won't you? The little time there is left. And talk to me. I can't let you go this way ... I won't let you go."

He put the paddle across his knees. But he said, "It's no use, girl. I'm sorry you feel the way you do, sorry it's hurting you like this. But there's nothing to be done."

"I've got to stop you!"

"You can't,"

"But—but why is it so important to you? I mean, I know you were hurt terribly, but what can you possibly gain by killing the man? Is it because—" She fell silent a moment. "Did you love the woman, Donavan? The one who was killed?"

And he was silent before answering. "Not in the sense you mean. I loved her as a man can love a friend. With more than affection, more than respect, but not the other."

"Tell me about her."

"Her name was Norma." Donavan could see little point in this, other than that to answer was to be kind, and perhaps that was point enough. "Norma Hamilton, and then Norma Murphy. A tall woman, not quite beautiful, dark hair, dark eyes. I remember her hands best, they were slender and very expressive. I met her in college, through her brother. We liked each other in the same way. There was always good companionship between us. Have you known anyone like that?"

"Not like that," she said. "But I wish I had."

"It was fine," Donavan said. "She was the best. What makes a good woman? Courage? Loyalty? Quiet but limitless strength? —she had all of these. And I think having so much of them is why she died. If she had been a little less—" It was a fruitless thought; Donavan dropped it. "It's to my eternal grief to know I was the one who introduced her to Jack Murphy."

"Who was Jack Murphy then? What was he?"

"I met him in Europe during the war," he said. "That would be World War II to you. We were in the same outfit, combat engineers. R.O.T.C. and my construction background had made me a captain, even at that tender age. He was a lieutenant. A big, lusty, free liver, very likable when he wanted to be; around me, he always did. He got in a little trouble, with our own people, and. I helped him with it. War nerves, I said then. I wasn't a missionary, I liked the man. And he knew construction. We came out together. I had Donavan Construction waiting for me; it was my father's before me. There was plenty of work, and room for Jack. I took him in, first as a superintendent, then as a full partner. The company grew very fast."

"Then Norma Murphy?"

"Yes. Perhaps because Norma and I were so much alike, she reacted to Murphy as I did. She didn't look deeper into the man than I did. She fell in love with the man she saw on the surface and she married him. She didn't think of marriage lightly. A marriage was a life's work to her, a sacred thing. You can hide a black soul from a business partner, but you can't hide it from a wife. Norma found it out soon enough. It was like her to try to change him, and go on trying, even after her love had died. She didn't try to hide the fact that her love had died—she was too honest for that—and when he found it out, her life became truly miserable."

"Why did he keep her?"

"It's the nature of the man," Donavan said. "Some are like that. Possessions are all important; they'll never part with one, they'll destroy it first. Norma was a possession, to be tormented, but not freed. Then he became sure Norma was in love with me. We met often. She honestly wanted to save Jack, and she always hoped that between us we could find a way. And we tried. But it was no good. Jack hired Hallock to follow us, and he made a record of our meetings, and the record helped to substantiate the overnight meetings they faked."

"How dirty can people get?"

"That wasn't the worst," Donavan said. "The worst came in a drunken brawl. Drink made him brutal and stupid. He threatened Norma's life. To make the threat real, he boasted of having killed someone else. Man or woman, true or false, I don't know. Norma didn't live long enough to tell me. She arranged the last meeting to talk about it, but she was dead when I got there. Jack had been there first, killed her to shut her mouth then framed her murder on me. And he was rid of both of us. I had to convert my share of the company into cash for my defense. He was glad to buy me out at his figure. Since then, I understand, he's done very well."

Elizabeth's voice was shaking. "And I thought Peebles was rotten! A dozen little Peebles couldn't match this Murphy. But don't you see? He's got to pay for his crime. We've got to see that he does."

"I intend to make him pay," Donavan said. "He'll be at the moorage that used to be my moorage—I'll collect from him."

"But not that way!" Elizabeth said. "Not at the cost of your life, too! You've got to tell the authorities what the truth is. They'll see that he pays."

Tiredly, Donavan said, "We go in circles. I tried, girl. I spent everything I had, and borrowed more; I used my friends and every other means I could think of. And I was able to convince the authorities of exactly nothing."

"We'll try again—with my money and my friends!"

Donavan was silent. Then: "You mean that, girl. I know you do. But I don't know why you should feel this way. I—" A note of uncertainty had crept into his voice; he stopped it. "You must be mistaken. You've known me only ... how long?"

"A thousand years!" she said fiercely.

His voice turned husky. "No...."

"Yes!" she said. "Listen to me, Donavan. I admit to you I'm a virgin. I've never even had a close male friend. And I'll admit I've been afraid of men. I've been taking postgraduate work, because college was a refuge for me. The longer I could hide away, the longer I could avoid facing the realities of life. It's the truth. You can use it to say I don't know what I'm talking about—without experience I'm not qualified to know how I feel, or know if what I feel is truly important or not. Go ahead and say it! But I'll call you a liar. I don't need experience to know what you mean to me. My heart tells me. I need you, Donavan. Now and forever."

Donavan could say nothing.

She said, "Don't lie to me now. And don't say anything just to be kind. Tell me ... don't you feel anything about me?"

Very quietly, Donavan said, "Nothing at all."

"Donavan ..."

"I'm nothing," he said. "I can offer nothing. Have I any right to ask anything of you? Or even think about it?"

Elizabeth's voice lifted suddenly. "You see! You see! There it is again. That's the kind of man you are, you blind fool! You're not a murderer! You—" The child awakened and stirred restlessly in her arms. Elizabeth held her tightly and silently until the child quieted again. "Oh, Lord," she said helplessly. "I've never wanted to scratch a man's face so much in all my life!"

"I know how you feel."

"But you won't change?"

"It's not possible. A good woman was killed. I'm the only one who'll do anything about it. And the only one who has nothing to lose by doing it."

"You have everything to lose!"

"In your judgment," Donavan said. "Not in mine."

Elizabeth made an angry sound. "Why do you want to do it? Is it a matter of honor? Revenge? Or in some idiotic way do you call it a public duty? What is your reason?"

"I don't think about it too much," Donavan said. "I see Norma's face. I hear her saying, 'We've got to help him ... there must be a way.' And that's enough. This is the woman he killed. He's got to pay for it. It's true that if I didn't make him pay no one else would, but it wouldn't be honest to say that's my reason. I'd feel cheated if someone else did the job. I want to do it. And I want nothing else under the sun."

"I can't stand it when you talk like that!"

"Then we'd best not talk at all."

Donavan took up the paddle again and began to use it, adding a little to the speed of the boat. Elizabeth knew a complete despair. The big, quiet man's mind was irrevocably fixed. She could think of no other argument, no other plea. She sat silent with the child against her breast, watching the steady swing of Donavan's shoulders and, when the moon gave light enough, searching his shadowed face for some sign of relenting or weakening. There was none.

They passed the lights of Johnsonville well offshore. Immediately below it, Donavan set a slanting course that would take them to the earliest high ground. The presence of the child had worked against him. Now he couldn't put Elizabeth ashore two or three miles below Johnsonville, as he'd intended. The child was too much a burden; the child needed care. He came to the shore in a wooded area and held off until he found open ground. Here he beached the boat, wading to the bow, pulling it above the water line. And he helped Elizabeth and the child to firm ground.

"Come with me," she said.

"You'll have rough going for a ways," Donavan said. "It's up hill and broken farm country. Go straight away from the river. The highway runs along the crest up there, half a mile away, maybe a little less. If you come into any kind of road or lane, follow it. They all go to the highway."

The child was awake again, though drowsy and limp with weariness. Elizabeth held her in her arms. She was not conscious of the child's weight, or the warmth of the small face against her neck; she was aware only of her failure. And the loss. He was close to her and she could see his face, but she could read nothing there. His face was closed against her.

"How can you do this to me?" she asked.

His voice was steady. "It isn't what you think it is. You've had a bad time. You're feeling things, seeing things that don't exist. You'll know it in a few days."

"It's not so!"

"Make it so."

"I can't," she said. "And neither can you. Donavan, give it up. There can be a lot for both of us, if you do. I'll do anything, everything for you ... for the rest of my life. There'll be happiness for you. I know there will."

He turned away.

"Then listen," she said. "When you leave, I'm going straight to the police. I'll tell them all about you, and all about what you're going to do. I have to. There's nothing else I can do."

"I know that."

"They'll be there before you, waiting."

"It's a possibility."

"It's certain," she said. "But even if it weren't, even if you did get there first and did what you want to do, there'd be no chance of your getting away. The moment they know he's dead, they'll know you did it. Because of what I'm going to tell them. I'll be the one who sends you to the gas chamber, Donavan. I can't do anything else."

He turned back to her, his big hands came down gently on her shoulders. "Anything is better than prison," he said. "Haven't I told you? If you feel you owe me something, this could be a way to pay it. My luck might run out, they might take me. If they do, don't let them give me another life sentence. Show them what I did was done with premeditation. Then, at the worst, they'll keep me only a little while in a cage." His big hands turned her. "Now go your way, girl. And I'll go mine."

She stood as he left her. She heard the splash of water as he floated the boat again, the thud of the paddle against the gunwale and the sound of the water before the paddle's deep thrust. When she turned, she could see only the dim outline of his shoulders against the shadows. He didn't look back. He drove steadily on into the darkness. Elizabeth's eyes were suddenly hot with the scalding of tears.

"Mother of God," she said. "Pray for him."

There was an enormous ache inside her, much despair, but not quite utter defeat. Wanting to stop him by any other means, she had not spoken of it, but she had never lost sight of one last fragile hope. If the police were to reach Murphy ahead of Donavan, if the police were humane and willing to lay a trap, Donavan could be taken alive before any crime was committed. The burden was hers. She had to find the police in time. She had to persuade them not to shoot on sight.

"Hang tight," she said to the child, and began running.

This was pasture land, long unused, with deep grass to tangle her legs, with hidden ruts and pits left by the hoofs of animals. She could not run fast for fear of falling with the child; the child, too small to run with her, had to be carried. The weight was not much at first, but with each hurried, climbing step up slopes slippery with recent rains, the weight grew. Soon, Elizabeth's heart was pounding violently and her lungs were filled with knives of pain, and squirming darts of brightness flickered before her eyes. She did not stop. She went on until the weight of the child and her failing strength had slowed her to a walk, and went on still until her legs betrayed her and dropped her to the round.

"You hurt?" the child asked.

Elizabeth hurt. There was a blade of pain driven deeply into her side, her lungs burned and her head throbbed enormously. The folly of hurrying too much was clear to her now. There was a long way to go—half a mile, Donavan had said. She would kill herself if she tried to run the full distance to the highway. Her strength had to be used sensibly. When she got to her feet and took up the child again, she walked. She would make herself walk when the way was uphill, and allow herself to run only when the ground was level and clear. It took strength to hold to this resolve with time so precious—a different kind than physical strength, but no more easily come by.

There was a fence with taut strands of barbed wire to bar her way. She could not climb through; she had to climb over, after the child had been set carefully on the far side. She left part of her jeans and some blood on the wire, and some tears of exasperation. There was a hidden ditch that held a foot of dead water, and she fell into it, twisting her ankle cruelly and bruising the child to crying. A plowed field was an endless sea of glue; wet soil, not quite mud, balled up on her overbig tennis shoes like leaden weights. And there was a brush-covered lot, where savage, clawlike limbs leaped out of the dark to rake her face; she was sure she wandered in circles here for an endless time. There was another fence and another ditch and finally a road.

Donavan had said all roads led to the highway. He wouldn't lie to her; not once in all the time she'd been with him had he lied to her. The road curved and curved again and went on and on, but in time she heard the bellowing of a heavy engine and saw the flicker of fast-moving headlights beyond trees. It was a truck on the highway, and in a moment it was gone and the silence and the darkness came back. But other trucks followed, and when Elizabeth reached the pavement, the first to find her weaving figure in the headlights came to a grinding stop.

The driver asked no questions; plainly Elizabeth could answer none. He put the child in the cab, then helped Elizabeth into the seat beside her. He ran to climb beneath the wheel and crowded the heavy truck through the gears, motor roaring.

"You're okay now," he said above the noise. "I'll have you and the kid in Johnsonville in two shakes. They got things pretty well organized—places to eat and sleep, hospitals, the works ..." His voice trailed off. Then, to no one in particular, his voice lifting, he said, "In the name of God, when is it gonna end? People can't take much more of this!"

Johnsonville was not a city. It could hardly even be called a town. But it was on the only high ground in many miles, and it had been swollen by refugees to almost citylike proportions. Every available foot of floor space beneath sound roofs had long ago been taken. Now the overflow was spilling out across the adjacent land where fields of tents were being erected under the brilliant, pitiless glare of emergency lights. There was bedlam here, and sorrow and courage and kindness and strength.

Men were working in deep mud, guiding trucks, unloading them, putting up tents, shoveling sand and gravel, carrying supplies—the yelling voices gave only direction, no urging was needed. Other men and women stood in patient groups, waiting for each newly erected tent to be assigned. Others waited in crawling queues before the bigger tents that were field kitchens and aid stations. Still others wandered aimlessly and alone.

The truck driver waved a hand at all this as they passed it, and spoke to Elizabeth with some pride. "Yesterday there wasn't nothin' here; tonight—look at it! Y'can't beat people like that. Nobody can!" He looked at her. "Feelin' better?"

"I was just tired," Elizabeth said. "And out of breath. I'm not sick or anything."

"Y'don't want to go to the hospital?"

"The police station. There is one, isn't there?"

"Sure," the driver said. "Sure, there's one. But they're busier'n the devil. You can see how it is—they got to patrol, they got to bring people in and try to find the missing—"

"Take me there!" Elizabeth said. "Please!"

"If it's important—"

"It is! It's—" Elizabeth stopped. She could not say why it was important; that was something she could trust to no one but the police. She said, "It's the child. She's not mine."

"Y'mean you found her? Where's her folks?"

"I don't know where her father is. Her mother's in a flooded house in Fieldview, beyond all help. But perhaps the father—I've got to report it, don't you see?"

"I'll take you to the cops."

He took her to a building in the center of Johnsonville. It had been a grange hall; it was a frontline command post now. There was a small crowd of men and women in the street before it—silent, numbed, patient. Elizabeth carried the child, and the truck driver made a way through the crowd for her to the door. A big man, wearing the mud-stained and wrinkled uniform of the county police met them here. A two-day beard stained his cheeks. He listened to the truck driver's explanation, his face sullen. His face was sullen because of weariness and pain seen, but to Elizabeth, frightened now, it seemed like brutal bad temper. The officer took the child from Elizabeth and held her to the light in view of the crowd.

"Any of you looking for one like this?" he asked.

There was a soft murmur, an aching sound from the crowd, but no real answer. The officer gave the child back to Elizabeth. "Come on in," he said. "Tell us what you know about her."

There were others ahead of Elizabeth, she had to take a place on a bench near the door and wait. This was a big room, long and wide. Near at hand, under the glare of gasoline lights, uniformed men were working at crude tables. There were field telephones, emergency switchboards, a shortwave radio. Farther back, in the shadows, were cots where uniformed men and others were resting or sleeping. About the whole place was a sense of urgency, of men trying to keep pace with an overwhelming problem. Every man that looked at Elizabeth wore the expression of a man harried and hard-driven. She could not find a single friendly face among them.

These were the police. These were the men who would go after Donavan if she sent them. Where was the humane one? Where was the one who would listen and understand? Where was the one who would say the life of Donavan, the escaped murderer who intended a murder, was worth the slightest effort to save? And now Elizabeth's courage failed her utterly. Donavan's life was in her hands. If she sent any of these after him, his blood would be on her hands—she was sure of that.

"You're next, miss," an officer said.

Elizabeth took a chair at a table, holding the child on her lap. The man across from her was a heavy-jawed, gray-haired man with bloodshot eyes. He was impatient and trying not to be. His voice had rough edge.

"Let's hurry it up," he said. "There's more behind you. What is it you want to report?"

"This child," Elizabeth said.

Her heart was sick with failure and with shame. She couldn't tell this man about Donavan. She told him instead about the child, saying she'd been floating in the boat alone. She told him, too, about the woman who was still in the house in Fieldview. The man smothered a curse.

"Fieldview!" he said. "I'd've sworn we got every living soul out of there. And in plenty of time. It was my job. I went around with a loudspeaker truck. I had the boys knock on every door!" He glared at Elizabeth with his bloodshot eyes. "How could a thing like this happen? Can you tell me?"

Elizabeth closed her eyes. "No, I can't."

Gruffly, the man said, "Sorry, Miss. I—well, forget it. D'you know which house it was? Did you get the name?" He wrote down the house number Donavan had given Elizabeth. "Smart girl," he said. "We'll find it. Now what about you? If you were on the river, you must have somebody lookin' for you?"

"Yes. My family will be worried."

"Your name?"

"Elizabeth Matthews."

The officer turned to call to a man at another table. "Speed! You got an Elizabeth Matthews on your list?"

"What's the name again?"

"Elizabeth Matthews!" He turned to Elizabeth. "What's your home address?" And when Elizabeth told him, he relayed the information: "Elizabeth Matthews. Route Three, box two-o-four, Biddleford. About twenty-two, gray eyes, blonde hair."

"I've got her."

"Hold that!" a voice from the back of the room said.

A man got up from one of the cots in the shadowed part of the room. He came forward into the light, rubbing sleep from his face, carrying a huge pair of army issue shoes. When Elizabeth saw the familiar lanky form, the lean face, the bald head, she almost wept with relief:

"Mr. Sharkey ... oh, thank God!"

"Lass, are you all right? They didn't harm you?"

"I'm all right. Donavan took good care of me. Mr. Sharkey I've got to talk to you ... It—it's terribly important. Can't I talk to you alone?"

"Right now?"

"This minute!"

"All right, lass. Come back here with me."

The man at the desk said, "Say, wait a minute. She—"

"Keep your shirt on," Sharkey said. "She'll be back."

Wearily, the man at the desk said, "Next ..."

Sharkey took Elizabeth and the child to the room that had been the kitchen of the grange hall. There was a single light here and, at this moment, no one near, awake or asleep. "Donavan didn't kill anyone," Elizabeth said. Sharkey, listening, knelt to put on his shoes. He was hard-faced and skeptical, and though Elizabeth was not able to convince him fully, Peebles' account forced him to go along with her at least part way. And when she said, "But he's going to kill someone, unless we stop him. He's going to the moorage to kill Jack Murphy."

"Good," he said. "This's the break I've been waiting for. I spotted you from that plane, I nearly connected with you on that island, but it got dark before I could find it, and you'd gone. Then all I could do was keep comin' down the river and keep hopin'. Now I know where he's goin', I'll be there waitin'." He started to turn away.

"Wait, please!" Elizabeth said: "Don't let anything happen to him. Promise me you won't! He hasn't hurt anyone; he's been hurt. We can prove he's innocent."

Sharkey was silent a moment, looking at her hard. Then he dropped a hand on her shoulder. "I'll do my best ... that much I'll promise you. But I can't guarantee you more. He'll be a hard man to take any way I go at it."

He left Elizabeth then. She saw him go by the cot he'd used, catching up a leather jacket and a rifle. The sight of the rifle brought fear back. Rifles were made for killing. Carrying the child, she went after him. He stopped at another desk; she heard him speak to a lieutenant. "I've got a finger on one of my convicts. He's a murderer and he's got another murder on his mind. I need a car from the pool."

"Take the nearest," the lieutenant said.

Sharkey turned, his fast stride carried him toward the door. Elizabeth called, "Mr. Sharkey ... wait!" He didn't wait. He only paused to say, "You look after the youngster. I'll take care of Donavan." And he went out into the night. At the door, Elizabeth saw him get in a car, start it and drive away. She turned back to the man with the bloodshot eyes.

"Where can I leave this child?"

"We've got a nursery, like," the man said. "Sit down for a little bit, and one of the boys will show you where it is."

"I'm sorry," Elizabeth said. She sat the child on his desk. "One of the boys will have to take care of her." She kissed the little girl's cheek and whispered, "Be a good girl. I'll come and see you real soon...." She turned away.

The officer said, "Wait a minute. You can't—"

"I can," Elizabeth said. "A man's life depends on it."

CHAPTER SEVEN

Lebannon watched the flood level creep the last slow inches toward the predicted maximum in the first hours after dark, Friday evening, June 17th. The people here could say the worst was very near, and take heart in that they had found the strength to endure it. But in West Mills and in Biddleford, and in all the other cities and towns between the crest and the sea, the worst was still somewhere out of sight. The people there could only wait and pray that they would be equal to the need.

In these same dark hours, the convict Peebles, rode ahead of the crest in an outboard-powered skiff, going swiftly downriver. He cocked his head to the humming of the motor and grinned. It was a real outfit—a sixteen-foot boat, big beamed, brand new, bone dry. After the leaky scow of Donavan's, it seemed to him like the *Queen Mary*. There were even cushions for a man to sit on. And the motor—there'd been some changes made while he'd been doing his stretch in the walls. The last outboard he'd seen before he'd gone up had been as noisy as an airplane. This one, big and gutty, was quiet as a mouse, almost. All the power a man needed, and more. When he opened the throttle all the way the skiff really put her bow up and scooted.

"A real deal," Peebles said.

He wore hip boots, wool trousers, a red flannel shirt, still wet from a recent washing, and a fleece-lined hunting coat. The coat was too big for him, but he'd turned the cuffs back on bony wrists and belted it tightly around his waist. Nobody would notice the size of the coat; they'd be looking at the black and white armband that said, "DEPUTY SHERIFF," in big, black letters. With a fine boat, wearing an official armband, a man could go just about any place, no questions asked.

He took the gray skiff downriver, staying well out in the stream. There were lights on the hills, over there on the right. Johnsonville, probably. Donavan had said Johnsonville wasn't far ahead. Peebles wondered how the big guy was doing in that leaky tub. Donavan could paddle till his arms fell off and he'd still get to West Mills too late. The big guy didn't know it yet, but he was dead.

"Stone cold," Peebles said.

He'd hoped for a gun—no luck on that, but a man can't have everything. He did have a billfold, eleven dollars and more identification than he'd ever use. He had sandwiches and coffee, cigarettes, matches and a flashlight, a six-cell job that could throw a beam half a mile. That light had saved his neck, back in Fieldview, or whatever the name of the town was.

Donavan had dumped him in the river. Donavan had pulled out and left him. He'd had a bad thirty or forty minutes roosting on the flat roof of a car port, and then he'd heard the quiet thrumming of a motor. He'd yelled till his throat was raw—cold as he was, running out of muscle, he'd been ready to settle for a bed in anybody's jail. He's got an answering shout, and this gray skiff had come ghosting out of the dark between the houses, and the beam of the light had hit him in the face. Next thing, he was sitting in the bottom of the boat, a fleece-lined hunting coat around his shoulders, a cup of hot black coffee in his hands.

"T-t-thanks for the coat."

"You need it more than I do," the man said.

He was stocky and big-shouldered, but not tall. His name was Finucane, he said. Harry Finucane. He owned a service station and a little garage—correction, he owned the pile of junk that would be left after the flood got through. He was a special deputy, not that that meant much. Every man who owned a boat was a deputy these days. He'd been on duty for forty-eight hours without sleep.

"Rough," Peebles said.

"I wouldn't be sleepin' anyway," Finucane said.

He'd lost a son in the flood, Harry Jr., seventeen, a better hand with an ailing motor than his old man had ever been. The boy had drowned, trying to save a schoolmate, when an overloaded rescue craft capsized.

"Takes some gettin' used to," Finucane said. "We had a lot of plans." He eased the skiff down a flooded street. "You must be new around here," he said. "I don't recall seein' your face before."

"I just got here," Peebles said.

He told the man his name was Biancone—safe enough, the only Biancone he'd ever met had been a cop, a thousand miles from here. He said he'd worked on a farm, upriver, and had stayed too long trying to save the stock. He'd had a boat, until a log punched a hole in her side.

"Spare me some more of that coffee?" he asked.

"Sure," Finucane said. "That's what it's for."

He took the cup from Peebles' hand and filled it from a thermos jug. He talked about the hundreds who were missing, the thousands who needed help. He was a pigeon, this boy. A real, six-ply Honest John. He was out here all alone, loot in every flooded house, and he hadn't picked up a dime. And no questions. You could tell him anything, and he'd buy every word.

"How often do you report in?" Peebles said.

"I don't," Finucane said. "Unless there's a reason."

He took the skiff into a narrow space between two houses, the throttle closed, the motor only whispering. He probed the shadows with the light. Peebles waited until Finucane's broad back was turned, and then he shrugged the hunting coat away from his shoulders, reaching for his knife. He needed that coat with its armband—no use getting the coat messed up. He put the knife blade deep in Finucane's back. He left it there until the stocky man had ceased to move.

Now Peebles took the gray skiff downstream. Fieldview and Johnsonville were far astern; the lights of West Mills were just coming into sight. Peebles listened to the motor and grinned. He'd lost some time in Fieldview—half an hour, maybe longer, squatting on that roof. And he'd had to wash Finucane's shirt before he'd put it on. Call it an hour, altogether. He would still beat Donavan to West Mills with plenty of time to spare. The big outboard could eat up miles faster than a cat could lick up cream.

West Mills was almost abeam. The lower town was dark, but there were powerful lights in the center of the town and there were a few flood-lighted areas along the waterfront. The place was really taking a beating. There wasn't a wharf or a dock anywhere in sight; they were all under, and the water was high on the doors of the dockside sheds and warehouses. Peebles saw a few people, several small boats and two big river tugs, but that was all. And no one hailed him. A dark bridge loomed up suddenly, and Peebles ducked as he passed under it. "A couple more feet of rise, and they'll have to open the draw to let a rowboat through."

He brought the skiff close inshore and turned downriver again.

Murphy's moorage was on the lower edge of town; he knew that much. All he had to do was cruise along until he found it. With maybe a million bucks' worth of equipment anchored there, it was an odds-on bet Murphy would be there with it. Peebles passed several lighted areas, and then he saw a scattering of lights where floating equipment carried the Murphy Construction label in letters big and black. Coming into it, he saw no one working, but he saw a lot of damage. A big rig—crane or dredge, he didn't know which—had broken halfway loose; swinging on a single line, it had smashed into other equipment, sinking some of it. A pile driver sat on the bottom, only the roof peak and the tall leads of it above water. Drift was jammed in everywhere; a strip of walkway was dangling downstream like a loose piece of string.

A long frame building—a floating dock, office and supply shed—was well lighted. Peebles swung the bow of the skiff upstream and came in to tie up at the wide mooring area. He'd had plenty of time to figure every angle, he knew just what he was going to do and say. First, he had to sell the idea he was Murphy's pal, but that was no big chore. When a guy rode a flood like this to tell another guy somebody was on the way to kill him, what could he do but open the door?

"A cinch," Peebles told himself.

Donavan had had his chance. He'd been too square to play it smart; too bad for Donavan. Now the squeeze was going to work a different way. Braced and ready, Murphy could cut Donavan down ... for free. All he'd get for knocking off an escaped con was a pat on the back from the cops. So then, by way of saying thanks, Murphy would ante up for Peebles. Money and clothes and a place to hide. But that wasn't half of it. As soon as the time was right, Murphy would ante up in heavy numbers. Peebles had the goods on him for killing his wife and framing Donavan; Murphy had to pay. Peebles could see nothing but smooth going ahead.

"As smooth," Peebles said, "as a she-mouse's belly."

He left the skiff moored to a ring bolt and looked around. There were plenty of outside lights on this building; he could hear a gas-powered generator going. He followed the wide walk around to the shore side of the building. The office was brightly lighted and empty. The door was not locked. He went in, waited a moment, then called out.

"Hey! Anybody around?"

"Yes!" a voice answered from another room. "What d'you want?"

"Murphy," Peebles said. "Jack Murphy."

A man came to the inner doorway. He was big, a sandy-haired bull of a man; his hands were black, his face unshaved. He wore caulked boots, stagged-off tin pants and a torn sweat shirt stained with grease. He needed a bath and his bloodshot eyes said he needed sleep. But there was no look of weariness about him; there was only a look of sullen fury.

"I'm Jack Murphy," he said.

Peebles said, "I got news ... news about Bruce Donavan."

"Donavan," Murphy said. "So what about him?"

"He'll be here in an hour or two."

"Donavan's in prison."

"He ain't now. They had him working on the Humboldt dike. The whole crew got washed out, a lot of 'em drowned. You know how Donavan can swim; all it did was turn him loose. He's comin' here, and he's got the idea he's goin' to kill you. I got here first."

"And who're you?"

"A friend of yours ... don't it look like it? I come a long way and took a lot a chances to give you this dope."

Murphy stared at Peebles silently, the look of sullen fury still unbroken. "Friend of mine, eh?" he said at last. "All right, friend. Come in here and tell me about it."

He led the way into the other room. It was a long room, a supply shed and workshop. Here were coils of bright new Manila line, reels of cable, oil drums; tools were stacked in every corner. Bins filled two walls, except for window space. There was a long workbench; a sliding door opened on the river side of the room. Murphy took a bottle of bourbon from the workbench, tipped it up and drank deeply. Then the sound of a crash upstream, the splintering of wood and the grinding of metal, jerked his head up. He swore a deep and bitter oath.

"Listen to that!" he said. "Every time that rig swings it costs me another ten thousand dollars ... and there's nothing I can do about it." He lifted a blackened balled fist. "I could save it with a crew of a dozen men, but they left me! Every damned one of them left me!"

"Can't you cut it loose?" Peebles asked.

"Cut it loose, be damned!" Murphy said hoarsely. "That's two hundred thousand dollars' worth of crane. I'll see it on the bottom first!" He stared furiously over Peebles' head, listening until the crashing stopped, then his eyes dropped to Peebles' face. "What about Donavan?" he asked suddenly.

"Like I said, he's comin' after you."

"How do you know? He wouldn't tell you."

"Look, let's get it straight." Peebles' thin face was tight, his eyes behind his glasses were overbright. "These ain't my clothes, see? I ain't the law. I run into this guy. He's dead—heart failure, it looks to me. Anyway, he don't need his duds or his boat. So I took 'em. Y'see, I was a con, like Donavan. We celled together. I was workin' with him when the Humboldt dike went out. We came downriver together."

"When did you split up?" Murphy said. "Why?"

"Tonight," Peebles said. "Like you say, Donavan don't talk much. But he give me enough so I could figure what he was goin' to do. I don't want no part of any kill. Besides, I got me to worry about. I figure you'd be glad to help a guy that'd risk his neck to tell you what was comin'."

"Help you?" Murphy said. "How?"

"Nothin' big," Peebles said. "Some clothes and chow, a place to stay out of sight till the shoutin's over, and then a little getaway money. What d'you say? Is it a deal?"

"I'll think about it."

"That ain't enough," Peebles said. His eyes took on an ugly shine. "I got to have it yes or no. And let's take it by the nose, Jack. If the answer's no, you've got a hell of a lot more trouble than just Donavan."

"So ..." Murphy said. "What kind of trouble?"

"The kind I could make, if I wanted to," Peebles said. "But don't get me wrong. I'd rather be friends, I told you that. And I ain't askin' much. Nothin' beside what I'm doin' for you. Let's both play it smart and get along."

Murphy was standing with his back to the workbench. He leaned against it now, folding his big arms, staring at Peebles. "Maybe we will," he said. "But I like to know where I stand. What kind of trouble can you make for me—tell me that first."

"I'll tell you this much," Peebles said. "Remember Welch's jewelry store that got knocked over here in town, eight, nine years ago? A big score they said, fifty thousand. It was closer to twenty-five—I know, because me 'n' Buck Harris, a safe man out of Salt Lake, did the job. And who do you think fingered the job for us? Johnny Hallock. You know Johnny as well as I do. He's done a lot of work for you, hasn't he?"

Murphy tipped his head. "I knew Hallock."

"So figure it out for yourself," Peebles said. "It wouldn't be smart to get tough with me. I don't want to, but if I shot off my mouth, you'd be in trouble up to here. What's the sense of it? Let's be pals and get along."

"You know too much," Murphy said.

His expression did not change. There was no preliminary move, no warning, but he was suddenly and violently in motion. A distance of a dozen feet separated the men. Murphy's caulks bit into the planking and drove him across the space in long strides. Peebles squealed with fright. He had time to twist away, but not to escape. Murphy's big hand closed on the collar of the hunting coat Peebles wore. He jerked Peebles back, swinging him at the full length of his arm. Peebles' feet left the floor; he landed with a crash and a howl of pain.

But he was not hurt or stunned. A small man, with the quickness and agility of a monkey, he was able to squirm out of the sleeves of the coat and leave it in Murphy's hands. He ran to the far end of the room and turned. The heavy, narrow-blade knife was in his hand. Murphy threw the coat aside. There was no fear of the knife in his face, or even any acknowledgment of it. His face held a dark and sullen anger and nothing else. He walked toward Peebles. Peebles backed against the far wall, his eyes wild and afraid.

"I'll cut you!" he squealed. "I'll cut you good!"

Murphy did not even hesitate. The lack of fear in the big man, his complete indifference to the knife, drove Peebles to the edge of hysteria. He was afraid to close with Murphy. He darted to the side, jumped to the top of an oil drum, then to the bench. He tried to run the length of the bench to the door, but Murphy wheeled and was there before him. Peebles ran back. Again, Murphy stalked him. Peebles ran wildly around the room, scrambling over gear, throwing whatever came to hand. Murphy moved after him, unhurriedly, watchfully. He drove Peebles into a corner only to lose him, then drove him into another corner and caught him.

"No ... no!" Peebles screamed. "Please—"

He made a feeble effort with the knife, too frightened to be effective. Murphy caught his wrist. He raised it high with one hand, lifting Peebles off the floor. His big body blocked Peebles into a corner until he had twisted the knife from Peebles' grasp. Then his left hand caught Peebles by the throat, and he dragged the small man to the center of the room. Here again the left hand lifted Peebles high onto his toes. The right hand used the knife, driving it in under Peebles' ribs and cutting down. The knife was very sharp. Peebles was opened from rib cage to groin.

Murphy dropped him to the floor. His expression did not change from sullenness as he watched Peebles die. When the small man was gone, Murphy went to the sliding door and shoved it open. He threw the knife far out into the river. Then he went back and got the corpse by an ankle and dragged it out on the outside planking. Using both hands on the ankle, swinging his big shoulders, he threw the last of Peebles after the knife. And then, unhurriedly, he went back to the bottle of bourbon, drank deeply, choked and coughed and spat.

The planks were stained where Peebles had died, a crooked trail of other stains led to the edge of the outside planking. Murphy found a bucket and dipped water out of the river to sluice down the planks. The outside planking needed a number of buckets, the floor inside the building needed more. He had not quite finished the task, when he looked up to see a lean and silent man standing in the doorway. The man was holding a .30-30 rifle.

"Would you be Jack Murphy?" the man asked.

"Right," Murphy said. "And who're you?"

"Tom Sharkey. I'm a guard from the state prison."

Murphy's sullen, bloodshot eyes were on the rifle. "Come in," he said. "Have a drink, and tell me what I can do for you."

The truck driver had been kind to Elizabeth. She'd found him at the supply dump in Johnsonville, and he'd agreed to bring her along on his return trip to West Mills. But not willingly. "Look, miss," he'd said, "West Mills has got a lot of bad trouble. And it's gonna get worse. No tellin' what might happen to you, if you start knockin' around there at night. You're a lot better off here. Here, you're safe." Her answer had been, "If you won't take me, I'll keep looking until I find someone who will." She'd meant it; he'd waved her into the truck.

They were just coming into the outskirts of West Mills. Elizabeth was sitting forward in the seat, unconsciously trying to hurry the truck on. Her hair was uncombed, a smudge of dirt lay across one cheekbone; her gray eyes were wide and haggard, showing clearly the near-exhaustion she was stubbornly trying to deny. The truck driver looked at her and shook his head.

"I don't know what you're going to do," he said. "But I'll give you ten-to-one you don't get it done."

"You'd lose," she said. "I'll get it done—I've got to! Where do you go in West Mills?"

"Hickman's Wholesale Grocery. It's on Pine, between Third and Fourth. Is that gonna suit you?"

"You can't go any closer to the waterfront?"

"Maybe a few blocks, if I had to. I don't know how much of it's under water. A lot of it, you can bet." He looked at her almost angrily. "But you're not goin' down there?"

"I'm going to the Murphy moorage."

"Murphy Construction?"

"That must be it. Do you know where it is?"

"Sure. It's at the foot of Williams, ten or fifteen blocks below Pine. But dammit—" He broke it off, rubbing his face. "Pardon my French, miss. I can't let you go down there! It's plain darned foolishness. You'd never make it. Besides, there's no use even to try. All that will be barricaded off. The cops or the Coast Guard, or somebody'll turn you back."

"Oh, no, they won't!" Elizabeth said.

"Somebody's got to," the truck driver said.

Elizabeth pressed her lips together silently. She said no more; she sat tense and waiting. In a little while, the driver took the truck through a guarded gate in a high wire fence, into the brightly lighted loading area of the wholesale grocery warehouse. He'd been watching Elizabeth, but not closely enough. She didn't wait for the truck to stop. She opened the door and jumped out an inch ahead of his reaching hand.

"Wait ... miss! Dammit—"

Elizabeth was on her hands and knees on the pavement, the palms of her hands scraped and burning. She got up quickly and ran toward the gate. The truck driver yelled behind her. The guard at the gate, an elderly man, came out of his little house. He was slow-moving and slow-thinking; by the time he understood he was to stop Elizabeth it was too late. He couldn't brace himself, he couldn't get a firm grip on Elizabeth's squirming body. She fought free of him and ran with the speed of a frightened deer down the shadowed street.

Pvt. Ernest Yost was nineteen, Pvt. Leland Carpenter and Pfc. Paul Demke were twenty. Sgt. Orval Rayot was twenty-three. They were national guardsmen on rowboat patrol in the waterfront district of West Mills, just north of Williams Avenue. There were ship chandlers' shops, second-hand shops, heavy hardware and building equipment houses, a few restaurants and a few bars along these streets. All were dark and silent, standing in slowly rising water. The depth in the streets varied with the fall of the land from as little as a foot on Williams to as much as ten feet a few blocks north. The street lights were not working. The unreal quiet, the eerie pattern of faint moonlight and deep shadow had almost persuaded the men they were patrolling in a nightmare. They used their long-barreled flashlights often, their heavy rifles were always close at hand.

"Now are you satisfied?" Sgt. Rayot's impatient voice echoed oddly among the silent buildings. "We covered everything two blocks each way. You willing to call it off?"

"So what I saw was a fish, maybe?" Pvt. Yost asked. He was in the bow of the boat, Demke and Carpenter were at the oars, the sergeant was in the stern. "A fish with arms, awready, like a man," Yost said. "Sure, that's what I saw."

"Rock head!" Carpenter said. "You didn't see anything!"

"So okay!" Yost said. "I'm outranked! Do it any way you want to do it. What's it to me, if the guy helps himself in every joint along the street? I should care?"

Demke said, "If the guy was naked, like you claim he was, what's he gonna use for pockets to carry his loot in? Can you answer me that, Yostie, boy?"

"You're askin' for it! One more smart crack—"

"At ease!" the sergeant said. "And that means both of you. C'mon, get with the oars. We been here long enough."

The men at the oars had no skill; they used them awkwardly, lifting the blades too high out of the water, digging them too deep. But the boat was driven north along the street. They passed the dark, recessed doorway of a second-hand shop and did not notice the quiet ripple that moved the water there. And in the two minutes in which the water was perfectly still, they'd gone far beyond any possibility of seeing the second ripple that was set up as Donavan's head slowly emerged.

His forehead appeared, the short, dark hair plastered bang-like across it, then his eyes. He held this level until he'd found the searching beams of the flashlights far up the street, then cleared his nostrils and expelled the deep, long-held breath. He was smiling a little. No pockets for loot on a naked man—how about those kids? But he couldn't smile about their purpose. The boys were young, but they'd been trained, and it was certain they'd been ordered to shoot to kill.

The water was chin-deep where he was standing. He left the doorway in a shallow dive, surfaced, and began to swim toward Williams Avenue with a smooth, powerful, almost silent breaststroke. The old rowboat that had served him so well was far behind him, abandoned the moment he'd come into the West Mills waterfront. It had not been his choice to come into the city so far upstream of the Murphy moorage; it had been his only means of escaping a patrolling tug. Once in the city, he'd decided to swim, rather than paddle the boat, and the wisdom of his decision had been proven, just now, for the third time. He'd met two other patrols, and there could well be others still ahead.

And for him, too, the deserted buildings, the dark and empty streets had the unreal quality of a nightmare. When he turned on his back to float and rest, he could look up past the brooding buildings at the scattered clouds and the stars and the moon that was like a broken coin, and he could wonder what was the reason for all of this. What sins had been committed to warrant so much punishment? But it was a question that would not be answered until Judgment Day.

Short of Williams Avenue a block or two, he turned toward the river. Williams ran along the crest of a slight hill, and there was a possibility that it was still above the flood with traffic moving on it. He used an overhand stroke now. A growing sense of urgency, a feeling of "let's be done with it" made him take the greater risk for the sake of speed. He passed close by an iron foundry; the furnaces were cold and dark, no smoke came from the tall stacks. He passed through a railroad switching yard where freight cars stood in silent water, and walked along a trestle, wading in water knee-deep. There was a small rise of ground above the moorage basin. He stopped there.

The basin was no longer a basin, but part of the river now. The fleet of pleasure craft, the houseboats, the river service station—all these were gone. Only the Murphy equipment with its scattered, brightly burning lights was left. It was secured to the strongest dolphins; it had been best cared for thus far through the flood. There was much damage—Donavan watched the floating crane that swung on one line smash into a row of moored barges and sink one—but there was proof, too, that Jack Murphy had done very well the past six years.

The floating crane was new, the big river dredge, still secure to four dolphins, was new, and there were two new floating pile drivers bearing the Murphy name. Donavan looked for the equipment that had once been his, and found very little of it. The tugs were gone, most of the barges were gone. And it seemed somehow ironically fitting to him that the pile driver that had been the start of Donavan Construction—the start of all this—was sitting on the bottom, only the peak of the A-frame and the leads showing above the water.

There was a floating walkway between the shallow water that covered the foot of Williams Avenue and the well-lighted floating building that housed the office of Murphy Construction. Donavan didn't use it. He went into the water again at the nearest point, sank under it and swam beneath the surface. The current here was strong. One long-held breath carried him nearly a hundred yards, and he emerged only a few yards from the building. He closed the distance with powerful strokes, caught the wide walk that ran around the building and hung there.

He could hear only the rush and gurgle of the water around the floats that supported the building and the deeper mumbling of the flood far out. And he was concerned. Where was the yelling Jack Murphy? Why wasn't he fighting the river, or driving a crew of men to it? This quiet held the threat of failure—if Murphy wasn't here, where could he be found? Still, the lighted windows offered promise of a kind. Donavan rested until he'd regained as much strength as he could, knowing well that all his strength would be only just enough. Now, with a powerful scissor-kick and the lift of his big arms, he came smoothly and silently out of the water and onto the walkway.

With his back hard-pressed against the building wall, he looked around the edge of the office window and found the room empty. He moved along, his back still against the wall, until he came under the first window of the supply shed and shop. Jack Murphy was here. He was sitting on a stool beside the workbench, the bottle of bourbon at his elbow. The heels of his caulked boots were hooked on a rung of the stool, his hands held a .30-30 rifle across his thighs.

Tom Sharkey was lying on the floor against the front or office wall. A dark thread of blood ran from a cut on his bald skull across his face and into the shadows; the unnatural twist of his right arm said the arm was broken. His face, mouth open and eyes slitted, was turned toward the window Donavan was using. Donavan could not tell whether the guard was dead or just unconscious. Murphy was staring at the prostrate man, not watchfully but sullenly, as a man would stare at a corpse. His back was toward the open, sliding door.

Donavan went around the building. His bare feet made no sound, the spatter of drops that fell from his wet body and soaked cut-off trousers was lost in the voice of the flood. He came up quietly to the edge of the open door and paused. Sharkey chose this moment to regain consciousness, groaning. And Jack Murphy spoke to him.

"So you decided to come around. Y'know what I

think? I think you've been lyin' there doggin' it. I think you've been awake the last five minutes. I've been watchin' you."

Sharkey said, "Why didn't you do something about it?"

"I wanted to see how long you could take it. Lying there with a broken arm, faking you're out—you haven't got guts enough for that kind of work."

Not being a cursing man, Sharkey did not curse Murphy, but he managed to condemn Murphy to eternal damnation by other means. Donavan moved into the room on silent feet. Murphy's back was still toward him, his attention held by Sharkey's blistering wrath. The butt of the rifle was resting on one thigh, barrel high, held loosely by one big hand. Donavan reached across Murphy's shoulder and tore the rifle from Murphy's hands. Without pause, he turned and threw the rifle into the river.

Sharkey groaned with real anguish.

Murphy lunged off the stool away from Donavan, a deep curse exploding out of his chest. He did not see what had happened to the rifle until he had caught a heavy shackle out of a parts bin, turned and thrown it. The flashing steel struck Donavan on the shoulder. It would have deflected the aim of a rifle, it would have given Murphy a moment's time, if time had been needed. But there was no need. Donavan was naked, save for the rough shorts, and his hands were empty. Murphy took a deep breath, swelling his chest, and let it go.

"So you finally made it," he said.

"That's right, Murphy," Donavan said, and his voice was quiet. "I'm years late. You should have died one minute after Norma died. But you're going to die now, late or not."

"I don't think so," Murphy said. "I think you are."

Donavan moved toward Murphy. He had not changed his mind. This was still a thing that had to be settled with the hands. The memory of a good woman's lifeless face required it. He had to beat the sullen face before him until the flesh was pulp, then grip the throat, thumbs digging deep, until the last spark of life was gone ... the slow way, the brutal way, because only in this way could there be full retribution.

And Murphy came to meet him. The flood had robbed and beaten Murphy, and the savage was loose in him now, raging and thirsting for something to destroy in turn. And this was not a thirst to be quickly slaked. He, too, wanted the slow and brutal way; he was willing to exchange whatever pain he might suffer for the greater satisfaction of causing greater pain. He was not afraid of Donavan. Murphy had never known fear. He met Donavan in the center of the room.

The first blow was Murphy's, catching Donavan high on the cheek, a hammerlike blow of a maul-like fist. Donavan was rocked. He had made no real effort to avoid the blow. Evading punishment was not his concern; he wanted only to inflict it. His fists, made hard with years of prison labor, were well suited to the task. He clubbed his left into the side of Murphy's jaw, his right sank deep into Murphy's belly. Now both big men planted themselves solidly on wide-spread feet and began to slug each other unmercifully. They swung almost in turn, as if each was defying the other to do more and endure more than he.

Sharkey could only watch them. Sick with pain, knowing that the splintered ends of bone would come through the flesh of his arm if he moved it roughly, he was helpless.

There was no cleverness in the way the big men fought. They did not jab and parry and feint. Their way was primitive. It was a methodic clubbing of the face and body with rocklike fists. Donavan's nose was broken, blood from it splashed his chest. One of Murphy's eyes was closed, an ear was badly torn and he spat teeth from swollen lips. No man, however strong, no man, however savage, could withstand such punishment for long. And the savage man, if he were the weaker, would drop first. Murphy saw the truth in this and broke away. Not out of fear, not wanting to end it—wanting to win by any means at all. He stepped back and lashed out with a caulked boot. The steel spikes raked Donavan's leg from hip to knee, turning it red with blood that sprang from a dozen cuts. Donavan avoided a second kick. Murphy did not try a third.

Murphy backed away, his eyes swinging to the side in search of a weapon. A carpenter's claw hammer lying on the bench came to his hand first. He turned it and drove the claws at Donavan's face. Donavan went into the blow, instead of away. Murphy's forearm struck across Donavan's shoulder, the hammer was broken from Murphy's grasp. Now Donavan's big arms had Murphy around the waist. He heaved Murphy up and crashed with him to the floor. Again Murphy refused to match his strength against Donavan's. His caulks, slicking at Donavan's bare legs got him free. He rolled away and came to his feet.

He wanted a lethal weapon now, and he ran to a stack of tools in a corner and found it. When Donavan came erect, he saw a double-bitted ax in Murphy's hands. He could not contend with that barehanded. But there were other corners where tools were stacked, and a near corner held another ax, a mate to the one in Murphy's grasp. And they were equal again—two razor-sharp blades for each man, two three-foot hickory handles to swing them by.

Now the end was very near. One blow could be fatal, one miss could leave the way open for a fatal counterblow. This was not as Donavan had wanted it, but the choice had not been his. Both men held their weapons the same way. The left hand gripped the extreme end of the handle, the right hand was up under the blades. Held in this fashion, the handle would serve as a bar to deflect a blow, the blades could be used in short thrusts to cut. The long swing that missed and left the way open was too long a gamble. Neither man was willing to risk it yet. They moved together carefully, axes poised chest-high, and when a distance of three feet separated them, Murphy began to circle. He wanted some advantage; if not an opening, at least a moment with Donavan off balance. Donavan turned with him, watchfully waiting.

The room was silent, except for the sound of the flood and the heavy breathing of the men who held the blades. The light gave deep color to the blood on their battered faces, their eyes were locked, unwavering. Donavan had patience and control, learned behind prison walls; he could accept the risk of being struck, waiting for the moment of his striking to be clearly shown. Not so with Murphy. Murphy's savage heart had always hated waiting of any kind. He had no patience and no control. He charged suddenly with a short, jabbing thrust of his blade. Donavan deflected it, the handle of his ax, meeting the handle of Murphy's ax, holding the blade away. Murphy was thrown off-balance, and Donavan was able to sink the blade of his ax deeply into the junction of Murphy's neck and shoulder. As Donavan had known it would be, it was quickly over.

That night was remembered by Donavan and Sharkey and Elizabeth in separate ways. For Donavan, it was not a time of triumph. There was not even the satisfaction that should have come of knowing a promise had been kept and a debt paid. The man had deserved to die—that was true beyond any doubt. And Donavan had accepted an equal risk in the killing. But the account could not be balanced at all in this way, and Donavan came to know it. He would not forget this night in all his years.

For Tom Sharkey, it was a night of trial. Donavan

could have used the rifle to hold Murphy at bay, but he had thrown it away instead. Was not what followed murder, then? And yet, without Donavan's intervention, Murphy would have killed Sharkey, an officer of the law. How could the saving of an officer's life, by any means, be called a crime?

"I deputized you," Tom Sharkey told Donavan, "the minute I saw you looking in the window. There wasn't time to swear you in—I needed help bad. Murphy had killed one man—his blood was on the floor—and he was going to kill me as soon as he knew I was conscious again. You came in and you gave me a hand as an officer of the law. There'll be no quibbling about the way you handled Murphy. I'm going to say thanks to you I'm alive."

For Elizabeth it was a night of failure. A night of running down dark and empty streets, past cold, still buildings. Foot and boat patrols seemed to lie in wait on every street. They drove her from her path many times, and twice she lost the way. She found the last slope of Williams Avenue, finally. She followed the walkway to the lighted building, only to discover she was much too late. Jack Murphy was lying on the floor in a dark pool. Donavan had done exactly what he'd said he would do, and she'd not been able to prevent it. A night of failure.

But there'd been one moment she could treasure. It was Donavan lifting her after she had fallen in the office doorway, Donavan's quiet voice speaking to Tom Sharkey:

"She'll be all right, Tom," he said. "Don't ever be in doubt of it—this girl is a lot of woman!"

Donavan and Sharkey and Elizabeth remembered these things in their separate ways. Donavan splinted Sharkey's broken arm. He gave himself into Sharkey's custody and helped both Sharkey and Elizabeth to the nearest police. Sharkey took Donavan back to the state prison and saw to it that Donavan was paroled outside the walls, in the custody of Mrs. Tom Sharkey and her two small daughters.

And other things happened. Elizabeth's father, John B. Matthews, was an important man in the state. A word from him was enough to cause the authorities to bring J. S. Hallock under close scrutiny. Without Murphy's money, influence and strength, Hallock could not stand alone. His full confession brought the light of truth to the circumstances of Norma Murphy's death. The discovery of Peebles' body clad in Harry Finucane's clothes, the discovery of Finucane's naked body upstream from the Murphy moorage, and the sorting out of these identities did not come until much later, and it was no longer important then.

John B. Matthews was a stocky man of sixty, with gray hair and amused blue eyes. He called upon Tom Sharkey to bring Donavan to his home one evening. Matthews was a man who enjoyed things dramatic and he would not let such a moment pass until he had extracted the most from it. He made them wait to hear why he had called them until after dinner. Then in the library, with coffee and cigars, he made them wait a little longer.

Donavan was willing that it should be so. He had not been outside the walls too long, and moments like these he, too, wanted to savor. The taste of a good cigar, the feel of good gray flannel, the walls of a decent home, the company of kind people—these simple things were so important. He wanted to walk slowly, to be completely aware and miss nothing. He wanted to breathe deeply of this air of freedom.

"Sharkey," John Matthews said, "you're done with Bruce Donavan. In a professional way, I mean. Hallock's confession has been accepted. As soon as the courts can act upon it, and as soon as the governor can get around to it, Bruce will be given a full pardon."

Sharkey wore his cast-incased arm in a black sling; he winked at Donavan and smiled at Matthews. "It's a load off my chest," he said. "I wouldn't like the job of taking him back now. If I tried it, my wife and kids would start out hunting a new father for their family."

"I wouldn't blame them!" Elizabeth's mother said. She was a tall, striking woman, dark-haired and very positive. "And if you'd had to, John Matthews would have been another father without a family. Isn't that right, Beth?"

"It surely is," Elizabeth said.

She was sitting across the room from Donavan, slim and lovely, in a dress of crisp cotton print. There was real happiness tugging at the corners of her mouth and a shining eagerness lighting up her eyes. To look at her was to feel warmth, and Donavan looked at her often. There was much yet to learn about this new way of living, and much that had to be carefully thought about. But Donavan could not honestly doubt that soon enough he and this girl would make their way together.

John Matthews began to speak of other things. He had been inquiring into the means by which Donavan could regain at least part of the construction company that had been taken from him. His information was promising. A will drawn up when Donavan and Murphy had been partners was still in existence. Murphy, who had lived only for himself, had left no other. Listening, Donavan drew deeply on his cigar and was content.

Spring had been late this year. In February and March, rain drenched the coastal lands of the northwest, but static cold held the high country locked in a frozen grip. With the thaw, the flood came and worked its terrible destruction. But the flood passed and found its way to the sea in God's own time, and the water receded from the cities and the land. The homeless built their homes again and the separated found each other and the dead were committed to the grave. The living took up their lives again and went on as best they could. Few who had endured the flood would ever be the same again. But it is a simple truth that a stronger material than the human spirit has yet to be discovered.

THE END

Olney John Hawkins (born in Hamilton, Montana, on October 1,1910) and his brother Ward Chambers Hawkins (born in Vancouver, Canada, on December 29, 1912) started their writing careers contributing to the pulps, then joined up to write for the slicks in the 1940s. They wrote thrillers for the *Saturday Evening Post* and *Collier's* as well as crime stories for *Ellery Queen's Mystery Magazine* and *The Saint*. After a move to Los Angeles, they begin writing film and TV scripts, creating the show *Shannon*, writing and producing for *Little House on the Prairie* and *Bonanza,* and turning out episodes for such series as *Burke's Law, The Fugitive and Cannon*. Ward went on to write a science fiction series for Del Rey Books in the 1980s. After a long illness, John Hawkins died in Los Angles on August 27, 1978; and Ward Hawkins passed away a few years later on December 22, 1990, also in Los Angles.

BLACK GAT BOOKS offers the best in reprint crime fiction from the 1950s-1970s. New titles appear every month, and each book is sized to 4.25" x 7", just like they used to be. Collect them all.

Harry Whittington · A Haven for the Damned #1 ·
Charlie Stella · Eddie's World #2
Leigh Brackett · Stranger at Home #3
John Flagg · The Persian Cat #4
Malcolm Braly · Felony Tank #6
Vin Packer · The Girl on the Best Seller List #7
Orrie Hitt · She Got What She Wanted #8
Helen Nielsen · The Woman on the Roof #9
Lou Cameron · Angel's Flight #10
Gary Lovisi · The Affair of Lady Westcott's Lost Ruby / The Case of the Unseen Assassin #11
Arnold Hano · The Last Notch #12
Clifton Adams · Never Say No to a Killer #13
Ed Lacy · The Men From the Boys #14
Henry Kane · Frenzy of Evil #15
William Ard · You'll Get Yours #16
Bert & Dolores Hitchens · End of the Line #17
Noël Calef · Frantic #18
Ovid Demaris · The Hoods Take Over #19
Fredric Brown · Madball #20
Louis Malley · Stool Pigeon #21
Frank Kane · The Living End #22
Ferguson Findley · My Old Man's Badge #23
Paul Connolly · Tears are for Angels #24
E. P. Fenwick · Two Names for Death #25
Lorenz Heller · Dead Wrong #26
Robert Martin · Little Sister #27
Calvin Clements · Satan Takes the Helm #28
Jack Karney · Cut Me In #29
George Benet · The Hoodlums #30
Jonathan Craig · So Young, So Wicked #31
Edna Sherry · Tears for Jessie Hewitt #32
William O'Farrell · Repeat Performance #33
Marvin Albert · The Girl With No Place to Hide #34
Edward S. Aarons · Gang Rumble #35
William Fuller · Back Country #36
Robert Silverberg · The Killer #37
William R. Cox · Make My Coffin Strong #38
A. S. Fleischman · Blood Alley #39
Harold R. Daniels · The Girl in 304 #40
William H. Duhart · The Deadly Pay-Off #41
Robert Ames · Awake and Die #42
Charles Runyon · Object of Lust #43
Paul Conant - Dr. Gatskill's Blue Shoes #44
Asa Bordages - Murders in Silk #45
Darwin Teilhet - Take Me As I Am #46
Stephen Marlowe - Blonde Bait #47
Jonathan Latimer - The Fifth Grave #48
Andrew Coburn - Off Duty #49
Basil Heatter - Any Man's Girl #50
Day Keene - Acapulco G.P.O. #51
John P. Browner - Death of a Punk #52
Glenn Canary - The Trailer Park Girls #53
Jacquin Sanders - Freakshow #54

Stark House Press
1315 H Street, Eureka, CA 95501 (707) 498-3135
griffinskye3@sbcglobal.net www.starkhousepress.com
Available from your local bookstore or direct from the publisher

www.ingramcontent.com/pod-product-compliance
Lightning Source LLC
LaVergne TN
LVHW021238080526
838199LV00088B/4574